Look for more
heart-stopping stories from

FEAR STREET.....

The Perfect Date

Secret Admirer

Runaway

The Confession

Night Games

The Wrong Number

FEAR STREET

WHO KILLED THE HOMECOMING QUEEN?

R.L. STINE

SIMON PULSE

NEW YORK LONDON TORONTO SYDNEY NEW DELHI

SIMON PULSE

An imprint of Simon & Schuster Children's Publishing Division

1230 Avenue of the Americas, New York, New York 10020

This Simon Pulse paperback edition September 2022

Text copyright © 1997 by Parachute Press, Inc.

Cover illustration copyright © 2022 by Marie Bergeron

FEAR STREET is a registered trademark of Parachute Press, Inc.

All rights reserved, including the right of reproduction in whole or in part in any form.

SIMON PULSE and colophon are registered trademarks of Simon & Schuster, Inc.

For information about special discounts for bulk purchases, please contact Simon & Schuster Special Sales at 1-866-506-1949 or business@simonandschuster.com.

The Simon & Schuster Speakers Bureau can bring authors to your live event.

For more information or to book an event contact the Simon & Schuster Speakers Bureau at 1-866-248-3049 or visit our website at www.simonspeakers.com.

Series designed by Sarah Creech

Cover designed by Heather Palisi

Interior designed by Tom Daly

The text of this book was set in Excelsior LT Std.

Printed and bound by CPI Group (UK) Ltd, Croydon, CR0 4YY

10 9 8 7 6 5 4 3 2 1

Library of Congress Control Number 2022932428

ISBN 9781665927673 (pbk)

ISBN 9781439121252 (ebook)

MIX
Paper from
responsible sources
FSC
www.fsc.org FSC® C171272

WHO KILLED THE HOMECOMING QUEEN?

1

The drums echoed through the halls of Shadyside High. As Eva Whelan hurried toward the stairs, the deep, booming sounds thundered louder and louder.

Eva smiled. All around her, kids rushed toward the sound, eager to get to the gym where the band was tuning up.

Everybody loves a pep rally, Eva thought. *Especially this one. Not only do we get out of the last class of the day, but we finally get to find out who will be homecoming queen.*

Eva smiled again, feeling a surge of excitement. She turned a corner and began making her way toward the stairs that led down to the gym. As she hitched her book bag higher on her shoulder, a strand of her long, dark hair snagged under the strap. She paused to pull it loose.

"Eva, wait up! Eva!"

Eva turned and spotted her best friend, Tania Darman, waving to her over the heads of the crowd. "Wait up!"Tania shouted again.

Eva waved back, then scooted to the side of the hall. Leaning against a bank of lockers, she dug into her jeans pocket for a rubber band.

She watched her friend weave her way through the crowd. Tania looked great, as usual. Slender, with straight blond hair down to her shoulders and a pretty face with an open, friendly expression.

"Isn't this great?" Tania exclaimed as she joined Eva. "Everybody's so psyched!"

Eva pulled her thick, dark hair into a ponytail. "Don't tell me you're not."

"Oh, I am!" Tania replied, her green eyes sparkling. "I mean, I might actually be named homecoming queen. I still can't believe it!"

"I hope you win, Tania." Eva held up both hands. "I've got all my fingers crossed for you."

"Your fingers?" Tania tossed her hair back and grinned. "What about one of your famous psychic flashes? Can't you predict whether I'm going to win or not?"

Eva shook her head. Some of her friends thought she was psychic because she got weird feelings every once in a while. She could sense when something was wrong, even though she couldn't tell exactly what.

Like last week, when she and Tania went shopping for dresses for the Homecoming Dance. As they checked out one of the most expensive stores in the Shadyside Mall, Eva felt a sudden rush of fear. Everything seemed okay, but she felt jumpy the whole time they were there.

Just before they left the shop, every alarm in the place went off. And three other customers were arrested for shoplifting—by security guards posing as shoppers.

Eva didn't get these feelings all the time. But when she did get one, she trusted it.

Still, the feelings were just that—feelings. She couldn't predict what was going to happen. She couldn't look into the future.

"It doesn't work like that," she reminded Tania. "It's not like I have a crystal ball or anything."

"I know, I was just kidding," Tania replied. They began walking toward the stairs. "But you know what? I don't really care if I'm voted homecoming queen or not."

Eva stared at her. "Are you serious?"

"Well, I wouldn't turn it down," Tania admitted. "But really, I've had such an incredible year so far. So much has happened—Mom got remarried in July, we moved into this fabulous new house, I really like my stepfather, and I've got a great new stepbrother."

That's for sure, Eva thought. She had a major crush on Jeremy, Tania's stepbrother. Jeremy, with his chestnut-colored hair and shy smile.

She didn't know him very well yet—but she definitely wanted the chance to get to know him better.

"And there's Sandy," Tania went on. "I couldn't believe it when he asked me out. And now we're actually dating. I mean, he's only one of the coolest guys in school."

Eva nodded. Sandy Bishop, the smooth, good-looking captain of the football team, was definitely cool. Everybody agreed on that.

Including Sandy himself, Eva thought. *He knows he's popular and he loves having girls fall all over him. Still, he seems crazy about Tania. So what if he's a little conceited?*

"Being nominated for homecoming queen is great, but it really doesn't matter if I win," Tania declared. "Everything is perfect right now. Hey, I even pulled an A on that French quiz yesterday!"

Eva laughed. "I'm really glad for you, Tania. You deserve to be happy. But let's get down to the gym. *You* might not care who wins, but I do."

The crowd grew thicker at the top of the stairs.

As Eva followed Tania toward the top step, someone jostled her from behind. "Hey, watch out!" she called.

But she felt herself being pushed aside, hard. Her books began to tumble out of her arms, and her backpack slid off her shoulder.

As Eva struggled to catch her balance, she saw something out of the corner of her eye.

A blur of movement. A figure emerging from the crowd.

Two hands, reaching out.

Reaching . . .

Tania let out a scream. Eva turned—and saw her friend go hurtling down the stairs.

2

Tania pitched forward, her arms flailing in the air. Students cried out in alarm and leaped out of the way.

Eva made a desperate grab for Tania's sweater. Missed.

Tania skidded down a couple of steps, her arms still swinging wildly for balance. Finally she managed to grab on to the metal railing with one hand.

She swung out into the air, then pulled herself back, crashing hard against the wall.

"Wow. Are you okay?" someone asked. Tania nodded and tried to smile.

Eva rushed down the steps. "What happened?"

"It was my fault," a voice behind them said.

Eva and Tania spun around.

Leslie Gates stood at the top of the stairs, gazing down at them with an anxious expression on her face. "It was my fault," she repeated. "I slipped. I'm so sorry. I didn't mean to push you, Tania."

Maybe not, Eva thought, staring up at Leslie. *But if Tania had fallen and cracked her skull or something, you wouldn't be totally sorry, would you, Leslie? After all, then you'd have a better chance of being homecoming queen.*

"I'm so sorry, Tania," Leslie repeated, pushing up the sleeve of her red sweater. "Really. Are you okay?"

Tania swept her hair out of her eyes. "Yeah. I guess."

"Oh, good." Leslie let out a sigh of relief. "Well, see you in the gym." She turned and trotted down the steps.

Eva watched her as she hurried past them. Tall and athletic, with silky brown hair and a great figure, Leslie was Tania's biggest rival.

In more ways than one, Eva thought.

According to Leslie, Tania always got everything she wanted. Tania had more friends than Leslie. She was going on the senior trip to London in the spring. Leslie wasn't. Tania had her own car. Leslie drove her family's station wagon—when she got the chance.

And Tania had Sandy, the guy Leslie had drooled over for months.

Tania and Leslie used to be good friends, Eva knew. But Leslie became too jealous and broke off the friendship. Now she barely spoke to Tania.

Eva looked at Tania. "Are you sure you're okay? You crashed into that wall really hard."

"Did I? I didn't notice. I guess I'm too excited to notice anything." Tania straightened her sweater and patted her hair. "How do I look?"

"Great," Eva assured her.

"Okay. I'd better hurry and get into the gym. See you later." Forcing a smile to her face, Tania turned and hurried down the steps.

"Hey! Good luck!" Eva called after her.

She didn't really hear me, Eva realized. *She's too crazed. Too happy.*

How long can so much happiness possibly last?

As another bunch of students clattered past her down the stairway, Eva shivered. The laughter and shouts seemed far away, and the sounds of the band faded.

She felt as if a dark, chilly cloud had suddenly settled over her.

The sensation lasted for only a second. Then everything became bright and noisy again.

It wasn't one of my "feelings," Eva told herself. *I skipped lunch. I'm hungry, that's all. And excited for Tania.*

Nothing's wrong.

Nothing bad is going to happen.

Taking a deep breath, Eva walked down the stairs and joined the crowd streaming into the gym.

The band sat in one section of the bleachers, still tuning up. In front of them, Shadyside's cheerleading squad practiced one of their routines, leaping and whirling and urging everyone to chant along. The wooden bleachers shook as the crowd stomped its feet in rhythm.

There was a low platform in the center of the shiny wooden floor. Jason Thompson, who had been named homecoming king the day before, stood on the platform next to the football coach.

Behind them, Tania and three other girls sat in a semicircle of chairs. All four of them were smiling nervously and waving to their friends in the stands.

But there should have been *five* girls.

Eva studied the faces on the platform. Tania. Julia Moran. Mei Kamata. Dierdre Bradley.

But not Leslie.

Where is Leslie? Eva wondered. *She went down ahead of us, and now she isn't here.*

She quickly scanned the crowd. *Don't be stupid,* she thought. *Leslie wouldn't be in the stands. She's dying to be named queen. She should be up on the platform, acting as if the crown is already on her head.*

So why isn't she?

The strange, foreboding feeling began to creep over her again. Eva bit her lip tensely, then forced herself to smile as Tania waved to her from the platform.

Waving back, she edged her way through the crowd and began climbing the steps into the bleachers.

As she climbed past the band section, the trumpets blared in her ears. The music grew louder, then ended abruptly.

In the sudden quiet, another sound rang out.

A single, sharp, metallic sound.

A piercing blast that echoed off the walls of the gym.

A shot! Eva thought with a cry.

A gunshot!

3

*E*va's mouth went dry. The blood pounded in her ears.

A gun! she thought in panic. *Someone fired a gun in the gym!*

Terrified, Eva opened her mouth to scream.

And stared as a boy sitting near her pulled something shiny and metallic off the floor of the bleacher.

A crushed soda can.

Eva snapped her mouth shut, feeling embarrassed.

The guy just smashed a can under his foot. I've heard that sound a million times. Why did I think it was a gun?

Because I'm jumpy, she realized. *Because I've got a bad feeling about things.*

Well, get over it, Eva ordered herself. *So what if those feelings always came true before? They won't this time. Everything's fine—just look around.*

A flash of red caught her eye. She turned and saw Leslie running across the gym floor, smiling and waving. The crowd clapped, and Leslie's face flushed with pleasure. She climbed onto the platform and joined the other candidates.

Eva rolled her eyes. So *that's* what Leslie was up to. Waiting to make a grand solo entrance.

Shaking her head in disgust, Eva turned and began climbing the steps again. As she did, she caught sight of Keith Hicks. Keith—a thin guy with dark, wavy hair—wore his usual color, black. Black jeans, black shirt, black cap. The only colorful things about him were the shiny gold hoop in his left ear and the piercing blue of his eyes.

Eva grinned, feeling better all of a sudden. Not because of Keith, even though she liked him okay. But because of the guy sitting next to him.

Jeremy, Tania's new stepbrother.

Tall and lanky, Jeremy leaned his elbows on his knees and stared down at the platform. His curly chestnut hair gleamed under the lights as he listened to whatever Keith was saying to him.

The space on Jeremy's other side was empty. *Go for it,* Eva told herself. *Get up there before somebody else does.*

As the band started playing again, she trotted

up the steps, then edged her way across to Keith and Jeremy. "Hey, guys," she said, interrupting Keith midsentence.

"Hey, Eva." Keith gave her a distracted smile.

Jeremy smiled too, and a cute dimple flashed on the right side of his mouth. But then he turned and stared straight ahead again.

Sit down, Eva told herself. *Get his attention. Flirt with him a little.*

Then ask him to the Homecoming Dance.

Crossing her fingers that Jeremy didn't already have a date, she slid next to him and propped her feet on her book bag. "Let me guess," she declared. "Keith has been talking to you about movies. Right?"

It was an easy guess. Keith wanted to be a film director. He *always* talked about movies.

"Yeah." Jeremy nodded. "But I haven't been listening much."

"Thanks a lot," Keith muttered.

"Give him a break, Keith," Eva said. She leaned closer to Jeremy.

"I'm too tense to listen to anyone," Jeremy confessed. He pointed to the platform. "I really hope Tania wins. Do you think she will?"

Eva's shoulders sagged a little. *He's too busy worrying about whether Tania wins to pay any attention to me,* she thought.

"I don't know," she replied. "I hope she does too. But she won't be upset if she doesn't. Didn't she tell you that?"

Jeremy nodded. "Yeah, she did. But *I* still want her to win. She's my sister, you know? Well . . . my stepsister, but that doesn't matter. We've gotten close since my dad and her mom got married this past summer."

"That's great," Eva told him.

"It is," he agreed. "I guess it sounds weird. But having a real family is so awesome. I never really had one before. My mother died when I was a baby. And I hardly ever saw my father because he worked all the time. He stays home more now."

Why is he telling me all this? Eva wondered.

"Tania's happy about it too," she said. "That's one of the reasons why she doesn't care about being queen. She said so many good things have happened, it just doesn't matter."

Keith sighed loudly. "If this were a movie, the sappy music would start playing right now."

Eva reached behind Jeremy and jabbed Keith in the arm. "What's the matter? Don't you like happy stories?"

"They're okay," Keith replied with a shrug. "But movies need more drama."

"This isn't a movie," Jeremy reminded him.

"No kidding. Anyway," Keith went on, "let me tell you more about my video."

"What video?" Eva asked.

"The one I'm going to make," Keith declared. "The one that's going to get me a scholarship to film school. That's what I was talking about before."

He gazed at Jeremy, his blue eyes bright and intense. "Hey. You know what would make it a great video?"

Jeremy shook his head.

"If Tania would act in it," Keith exclaimed. "She'd be perfect, right? Do you think she'd do it?"

"Man!" Jeremy laughed. "You'll do anything to get close to Tania—won't you?"

Keith's face grew dark. He raked his fingers through his black hair and licked his lips. "Yes," he replied softly. "Anything."

Whoa! Eva thought. *What a weird thing to say. And what a weird look in his eyes. So what if he has a crush on Tania? How come he's suddenly acting so strange?*

"Hey, maybe I'll write in the video script that Tania dumps Sandy for me," Keith announced.

Jeremy snickered. "Why don't you just *murder* Sandy? That's the only way you'll get Tania to notice you!"

Keith's grin grew wider, but Eva thought it

looked fake. And his eyes! Why did they glitter like that?

Another chill raced up Eva's spine.

Ignore it, she told herself. *It doesn't mean anything.*

But the feeling didn't go away. She glanced sideways at Keith.

What is he thinking?

"Come on, everybody!" one of the cheerleaders shouted from below. "Let's hear some *real* noise!"

Eva dragged her eyes away from Keith and watched as the cheerleading squad began another routine. Everyone else clapped and cheered along, but Keith kept talking about the video he wanted to make.

"Leslie already volunteered to be in it," he shouted above the loud chanting. "She said she'd do the lead role, like it would be a big favor."

"Wouldn't it?" Jeremy asked.

Keith shook his head. "Leslie is desperate to be an actress. She's applying to every acting school in the country. If she's in the video, then she'll have something to show. I'd be doing *her* the favor."

"Sounds like a good deal for both of you," Jeremy commented. "Is Leslie any good?"

"Sure," Keith replied with a shrug. "But I'd much rather have Tania—especially if she's homecoming queen."

"What does that have to do with anything?" Eva asked. "I mean, what's your video about?"

Keith's eyes glittered again. "It's called *Who Killed the Homecoming Queen?*"

The cheerleaders finished their routine and ran off the floor, waving their pom-poms. Everyone clapped, then began to whistle and stamp their feet as the football coach picked up a microphone and asked everyone to quiet down.

Eva knew Coach Jackson was about to announce the name of the queen. But she couldn't stop staring at Keith.

Who Killed the Homecoming Queen? Why did Keith get that flash of excitement in his eyes when he told her the title?

Something's wrong, I can feel it.

But what?

"Only one more week until homecoming!" Coach Jackson's voice boomed through the loud-speakers. "And now, the name you've all been waiting for! This year's Shadyside High School homecoming queen is . . ." The coach paused dramatically. "Tania Darman!"

The gym erupted in cheers and whistles and applause. Jeremy gave a whoop and leaped to his feet. Eva stood too, clapping hard and craning her neck to get a glimpse of her friend.

Tania sat in her chair, looking stunned. Her mouth fell open. She raised her hands to her face.

The coach held up a sparkling rhinestone crown and handed it to Jason Thompson. "Tania, congratulations!" he boomed. "Now come on and let Jason put this crown on your head!"

Tania rose to her feet. The other candidates, who would be princesses in the homecoming court, rushed to hug her. All except Leslie, Eva noticed. Leslie stood to the side, watching. Waving to the crowd, Tania started across the platform to accept the crown.

Halfway to the podium, she stopped. Her arms dropped limply to her sides.

Then, as if a giant boot had come crashing down on top of her, she crumpled in a heap to the floor.

4

The cheers turned to gasps and screams.

Then a stunned silence fell over the crowded gym.

Eva stared down, frozen in horror.

Tania didn't move.

I knew it, Eva thought. *I knew something was wrong. I could feel it!*

"Hurry, Eva!" Jeremy cried. He lurched in front of her and almost tripped. "We have to get down there!"

Eva finally started to move into the aisle. Then she stopped suddenly, and grabbed hold of Jeremy's arm. "Wait! She's sitting up—look!"

Eva kept hold of Jeremy's arm as they both stared down at the platform.

Tania had braced herself up on one elbow. She brushed her hair out of her eyes and glanced up at the coach. He had shooed Jason and the girls out of the way and was bending over Tania.

Tania shook her head and said something. The coach held out his hand and helped her to her feet. Pale but smiling, Tania moved across the platform to the microphone.

"I guess you can see that being named queen really knocked me out!" she declared in a shaky voice. "Actually, some of you probably know I have low blood sugar. Sometimes a lot of excitement makes me faint. And believe me, being homecoming queen is definitely enough to do it!"

Everyone clapped and cheered.

Eva laughed with relief. She could feel Jeremy relax next to her. "I should have guessed what it was," she told him. "I've known about Tania's low blood sugar all my life, practically."

Down on the platform, Tania continued speaking. "As soon as I have some fruit juice or something else that's sweet, I'll be fine," she assured the crowd. "Not that being queen isn't sweet—it is. I'm really happy and grateful. Thanks a lot, everybody!"

Jason set the crown on Tania's head. Everyone clapped and cheered some more.

"Is this great or what?" Jeremy asked. "My sister, the homecoming queen. Come on, let's go down and congratulate her."

He grabbed Eva's hand and started pulling her down the bleachers. But as Eva reached back for her book bag, Jeremy's hand slipped away.

Eva watched him hurry down ahead of her. *Too bad,* she thought. *Holding his hand felt good.*

Finally Eva made it down to the bottom bleacher. As she jumped to the gym floor, she saw Jeremy race to the platform and give Tania a big hug.

It's great that they're so close, Eva thought. *Tania's boyfriend ought to be up there with her too.*

Where is Sandy?

Eva glanced around, trying to spot Sandy Bishop. But she didn't see him anywhere in the crowd.

Weird, she thought.

With a shrug, Eva started toward the platform, then found herself caught up in the middle of a huge group of kids hurrying toward the gym doors. They swept her along with them for a few seconds until she finally managed to pop free.

As she spun away from them, she bumped into Leslie Gates.

"Oops, sorry," Eva said, slinging her book bag over her shoulder.

Leslie nodded, then quickly turned away.

But Eva saw the gleam of tears in her eyes.

"Hey, Leslie." She reached out and touched her arm. "Are you crying?"

"Of course not." Leslie's voice shook, and she kept her head turned away. "I have something in my eye."

Sure, Eva thought. As she watched Leslie trying to blink an imaginary piece of dirt out of her eye, Eva couldn't help feeling sorry for her.

Okay, so she dropped Tania because she's jealous of her, Eva told herself. *So she's kind of a snob. But she is obviously hurt.*

"Listen, Leslie," Eva murmured. "Try not to feel so bad, okay? It's not the end of the world."

"I know that. It's just . . ." Leslie wiped her eyes and took a shaky breath. "It's just that Tania gets everything she wants—and I get nothing. She's Miss Perfect. The Golden Girl of Shadyside High."

"That's not true," Eva argued. "Things don't always go right for her. I mean, her parents got divorced two years ago. She and her mom had to move to that horrible apartment in the Old Village—remember?"

"Yeah, but her mother remarried, and they moved into a great house, and Tania has a cool stepbrother and they're just one big happy family!" Leslie shot back. "*Plus,* Tania gets to be homecoming queen!"

And she also gets Sandy Bishop, Eva thought. But she didn't say it. Leslie would probably freak if she did.

"You can't blame Tania just because she got the most votes," Eva told her. "Besides, you're not the only one who didn't win."

"Gee, thanks for the lecture, Mom."

Eva sighed. "It's no good being jealous, Leslie."

"Oh, shut up!" Leslie snapped. "Go be Tania's best friend and leave me alone!"

Tossing her hair back, Leslie turned and pushed her way through the crowd to the exit doors behind the bleachers.

Eva gritted her teeth and went after her. *I don't care if she thinks I'm lecturing her,* she thought. *I have to try to make her stop hating Tania so much. Something bad will happen if she doesn't.*

Maybe that's the bad feeling I've been getting— Leslie's hatred.

As Eva reached the back of the bleachers, she caught a glimpse of Leslie's red sweater. Leslie went speeding through the doors. Eva hurried to catch up before Leslie got too far ahead.

Then something behind the bleachers caught her eye. She stopped suddenly, turning her head to look.

And she gasped in shock.

5

*E*va clapped a hand over her mouth and quickly ducked back behind the bleachers.

Did I really see that? she wondered.

Slowly she peeked around the corner and stared.

Sandy Bishop stood in the dim, narrow space between the bleachers and the back wall of the gym. Sandy, Tania's boyfriend. Tall and athletic, with wide shoulders and thick, shiny hair that matched his name.

Sandy didn't see Eva, of course. His eyes were closed. He was kissing a girl who leaned against the wall. The girl's eyes were closed too.

And she wasn't Tania.

This girl was short, with bright coppery hair that floated around her head in a mass of waves and curls. Only one girl in their class had hair like that—Cherise Colby.

Eva's heart dropped as she watched Cherise stand on tiptoe and wrap her arms more tightly around Sandy's neck.

But he's supposed to be crazy about Tania! Eva told herself. *Why is he hiding behind the bleachers, kissing Cherise?*

Stupid question, she decided. *He's kissing Cherise because he obviously* isn't *crazy about Tania.*

And Tania doesn't have a clue.

Not yet, anyway.

But people would find out. Sandy couldn't keep it a secret forever. Cherise would say something to a friend. And the friend would tell someone else. And eventually the news would get around to Tania.

What an awful way to find out.

Eva bit her lip. *Should I tell her? After all, I'm her best friend. It wouldn't make it any easier for her. But at least she wouldn't find out through whispers.*

Should I tell her the bad news?

Or should I keep it from her?

Eva chewed her lip, not knowing what to do. If she didn't tell Tania, it would be like lying. But telling her would be so hard.

Down the shadowy passageway, Sandy and Cherise finally broke their embrace and gazed into each other's eyes for a moment. Then they began kissing again.

Eva ducked away. She'd seen enough.

The question was, what should she do about it?

Feeling sad and furious at the same time, Eva turned to the gym doors.

But someone blocked her way.

Leslie. She had come back, and now she stood a few feet in front of Eva, staring at Sandy and Cherise. She watched them for another second, then slowly turned to Eva.

Leslie's eyes were shining again, but not with tears. This time, they shone with glee.

"This will *kill* Tania!" Leslie declared triumphantly.

6

After school the next afternoon, Eva stood near the bleachers at the football stadium, watching Tania and Sandy argue with each other.

Tania looks angrier than I've ever seen her, she thought. *And the way Sandy keeps clenching his fists! It's really frightening.*

A sudden gust of wind blew a strand of hair across Eva's face. Her nose itched and her eyes watered. She needed desperately to sneeze.

But if I do, they'll notice me, she thought. *And who knows what might happen then?*

"Come on, Tania." Sandy's voice sounded impatient. "I don't have a clue what you're talking about."

"Give me a break!" Tania cried. "You know exactly what I'm talking about. Do me a favor and stop pretending you don't."

"I'm not pretending!" Sandy took a deep breath and shoved his fists into the pockets of his jeans. "I don't feel like playing guessing games, Tania. Why don't you just tell me what's going on?"

Ha, Eva thought. *As if you don't know.*

Tania's green eyes narrowed to slits. "Okay, Sandy, I'll tell you. I found out the truth. I found out that you've been sneaking around on me."

Sandy frowned in confusion. "What?"

"Seeing somebody else," Tania snapped. "That's what 'sneaking around' means, Sandy. You've been seeing somebody else—behind my back!"

"No." His fists came out of his pockets and he reared back, looking outraged. "That's a lie!"

"It's true!" she shouted. "I saw you! And I have friends, Sandy. They saw you too."

"It's a lie," he repeated, shaking his head furiously. "I don't care what you and your friends *think* you saw!"

"Oh, please!" Tania rolled her eyes.

"I'm *not* seeing anybody else, Tania. You and your friends are totally wrong."

Tania crossed her arms and gazed at him furiously.

Sandy stared back at her, a scowl on his face.

Eva watched them, not daring to move. *What's going to happen?* she wondered.

Finally Tania sighed. "Look, this is crazy."

"You got that right," Sandy agreed quickly. He stepped toward her, his arms out as if to hug her.

"No." Tania moved back, shaking her head. "I mean it's crazy to keep arguing. I know what I saw. And so do my friends."

She took a long breath. Her green eyes seemed to fill with tears. "It's over, Sandy."

"What's that supposed to mean?"

"You want me to spell it out?" she asked. "Okay—I'm breaking up with you. It's over. Get it now?"

"You can't!" Sandy's voice rose. His fingers squeezed into fists again. "You can't break up with me. Not before the Homecoming Dance."

"You should have thought of that *before* you decided to fool around with somebody else," Tania told him. "I'm the homecoming queen, remember? I'm not going to that dance and looking like a fool. If you want to go so much, then why don't you take your *new* girlfriend?"

"I'm telling you—it's a lie!" he insisted.

"Give it a rest, Sandy!" she snapped. "Everyone in school knows the truth about you!"

"You can't do this!"

"Guess what? I just did!" Tania swept her hair out of her eyes and started to stalk away.

Sandy grabbed her arm and spun her around to face him. "You think you can break up and then walk away from me, just like that?" he asked angrily.

Glaring at him, Tania tried to peel his fingers off her arm. "Let go, Sandy!" she ordered through clenched teeth.

Sandy tightened his grip and shook her.

Tania's head whipped back.

Eva gasped. *He's going to hurt her,* she realized.

"Let go!" Tania screamed.

She swung her free arm up to slug him. But Sandy grabbed that one too.

"I'm not letting you go!" Sandy roared furiously. "I'll never let you go!"

"Stop it, you're hurting me!" Tania screamed.

Eva saw Sandy's hands reach up and grip Tania's shoulders. His eyes blazed with rage. He shook her viciously, back and forth, until her head wobbled like a rag doll's.

He'll kill her! Eva thought. *He's crazy!*

"Stop!" she shouted. "Sandy, stop it!" She started toward them.

Sandy kept shaking. Harder and harder.

Twisting in his grip, Tania finally managed to crash her fist into the side of his head.

Sandy staggered and stared at her, blinking in

pain. Then he lunged at Tania. His hands circled her throat.

"What are you doing?" Tania shrieked. "You're choking me! Stop it! Stop!"

He's killing *her!* Eva thought desperately. *Sandy's killing her. I have to stop him!*

Tania's cries turned to horrible strangling sounds. Her eyes bulged. Her arms dropped limply to her sides and her knees buckled.

Eva stared in horror as Tania slumped lifelessly to the ground.

"No!" Eva screamed into the silence. "Nooo!"

7

*C*ut!" Keith shouted. "That was excellent! Take a couple of minutes, everybody!" He straightened up from the video camera.

Eva watched Tania roll onto her back and stare up at the blue October sky.

Sandy strolled away from her, flexing his hands and grinning to himself.

Eva sneezed loudly, then sat cross-legged in the grass and sighed. They'd already done the scene three times.

It had been fun at first, but now she felt a little bored. And hungry.

"Eva, that was an *excellent* scream," Keith told her. "Really gave me the creeps."

"Thanks." It gave *her* the creeps too. The entire story did.

"The whole scene went very well, guys," Keith

announced. "Unfortunately, we have to do it again."

"You're kidding." Sandy wheeled around. "What for?"

Keith pointed to the sky. "Check out the plane."

Eva glanced up and saw a small silver plane gliding overhead. She hadn't noticed it before, of course. But now she could hear how loud it was.

"I don't want that on the soundtrack," Keith explained. "And there's no way to keep it off except to wait until it goes by."

Sandy groaned.

Keith shrugged. "Hey, that's an outdoor shoot. What can you do?"

"So why don't we shoot indoors?" Sandy demanded. "It would make things a whole lot easier."

Keith shook his head. "Lighting rooms can be tricky. Besides, I wrote the thing for outdoors, and that's where I want to record it."

"Great!" Sandy rolled his eyes. "I don't know if I can top the performance I just gave."

Eva sighed. *Mr. Conceited,* she thought. *The first video Sandy has ever been in, and suddenly he's acting like he's Brad Pitt!*

"Give us a break, Keith!" Sandy argued. "Play the video back. Maybe the plane noise isn't on it."

Keith pointed to the headphones slung around

his neck. "I already heard it, loud and clear," he replied. "Would you stop griping, Sandy? Let's do the scene again before something else goes wrong."

With a scowl and a huge, dramatic sigh, Sandy began moving toward Tania, who still lay on her back. "Come on, Tania," he told her. "Let's get this over with. If we're lucky, we might actually be finished by morning."

Tania didn't move.

"Hey, Tania, get up. Tania?" Sandy dropped to his knees beside her.

"Hey!" he cried. He turned to Eva, his face twisted in panic.

"Something's really wrong with Tania! She isn't moving!"

8

She's not moving!" Sandy cried frantically. "She won't wake up!"

Eva and Keith raced to Tania's side. Before they reached her, Sandy grabbed her by the shoulders and tried to pull her into a sitting position.

"Tania, wake up!" he cried hoarsely. "Wake up!"

Tania's head flopped back as Sandy shook her.

"Stop it, Sandy!" Eva shouted. She dropped to the grass and cradled Tania's head in her hands. "Let her back down! You're going to hurt her."

"Oh, wow!" Sandy quickly let go. As Tania fell back against Eva, Tania moaned softly and her eyelids fluttered.

"Look, she's coming around," Keith murmured. "Hey, Tania. What happened? You okay?"

"Of *course* she's not okay! Are you nuts or

something?" Sandy snapped angrily at Keith. "Don't just stand there. Call for an ambulance!"

"Sandy, shut up!" Eva cried. "Tania just said something. You're yelling so loud, you didn't even hear her!"

Sandy scowled, then bent over Tania. "What is it?" he asked. "What's wrong, Tania?"

"I said 'no ambulance,'" Tania whispered. "I'd die of embarrassment. I don't need a doctor."

"But . . ."

"It's just the blood sugar thing," Tania choked out. "Too much excitement again, I guess."

Eva sighed with relief. "Anybody got some juice?" she asked. "Or soda?"

"Yeah. I have a Pepsi in my backpack," Keith replied.

"Well, get it!" Sandy snapped.

Keith hurried to his pack, fished out the can of soda, and brought it back.

Tania sat up and drank it quickly. "That's better," she announced. Then she started to get to her feet.

"Whoa, not so fast!" Sandy told her. "Just sit here for a while. You're still so pale, you know."

Tania laughed. "So are you, Sandy. Haven't you ever seen anyone faint before?"

"Not somebody I care about." Sandy dropped

next to her in the grass and slipped an arm around her shoulders. "You really gave me a scare. I don't know what I'd do if something really bad happened to you."

You'd run straight to Cherise for sympathy, Eva thought in disgust. *And she'd give you plenty of it.*

"I'm fine," Tania assured Sandy. "But thanks for being so worried."

Sandy smiled and pulled Tania closer to him.

Eva felt like gagging.

What a two-faced creep he is! she thought. *Putting on this big dramatic act of caring about Tania. Acting as if she's the most important person in the world to him.*

And all the time he's sneaking around with somebody else.

It's like Keith's video come true, she thought.

There's just one difference—Tania doesn't know what a phony Sandy is. She doesn't know about Cherise.

I have to tell her, Eva decided as she watched Sandy help Tania to her feet. *Sandy has her fooled. She thinks he's the greatest guy in the world.*

She should know the truth about him. And I have to tell her.

"Okay!" Keith cried as Tania brushed blades

of grass from her jeans. "Is everybody ready for another take?"

"Keith, I can't," Tania declared, glancing at her watch. "I have to be in the auditorium in ten minutes. I have a rehearsal for the homecoming ceremony."

"This won't take long," Keith insisted. "You've got the lines down cold. And the last take was perfect except for that plane."

"I know, but . . ."

"Besides, I don't have forever to do this video," Keith pleaded. "It's October. We've been lucky so far, but the weather could change any day."

"Hey, give her a break," Sandy told him. "She can't stay. It's not her fault."

Tania laughed. "Actually, it is. If only I hadn't fainted."

As Keith ran a hand through his hair in frustration, Tania grabbed it and gave it a squeeze. "I'm sorry, Keith. I promise not to faint next time."

Blushing, Keith gave her a lopsided grin.

Jeremy's right, Eva realized. *Keith has a major crush on Tania.*

Tania gave Keith's hand another squeeze, then turned to Sandy and kissed him quickly on the cheek. "See you later."

As Tania ran down the hill toward the school,

Eva grabbed her book bag and followed.

Now's my chance to tell her about Sandy, she thought. *I'll just tell her and get it over with. It won't be fun, but at least she'll know the truth about him.*

I just hope she won't be mad at me *for telling her,* Eva thought.

Picking up her pace, she caught up to Tania as she was about to enter one of the side doors of the auditorium.

"Hey, Tania. Can I talk to you a minute?"

"Sure." Tania shoved open the door, and they stepped inside. "What is it?"

"I—"

"Whoa, it's pitch-black in this place," Tania interrupted as the heavy door clanged shut behind them. "I guess I'm the first one here. Where's a light switch?"

"I'm not sure." Eva blinked, waiting for her eyes to adjust. They stood in one of the side aisles, next to the back row of seats. "I guess we could turn the stage lights on. But why don't we sit down and talk?" she suggested, pointing to the seats.

"Sure, but let's get some light in here." Tania began walking down the carpeted aisle toward the stage. "What do you want to talk about?"

Eva frowned, trying to decide how to start.

Should I just blurt it out? Guess what? Sandy's fooling around with Cherise.

"Eva?" Tania's voice came from farther down the aisle. "What is it?"

"Well . . ." Eva slowly started toward the stage. This was harder than she'd thought it would be.

"Is everything okay?" Tania asked. Her sneakers squeaked as she began climbing the wooden steps leading up to the stage. "You seem awfully worried about something."

"I am, sort of," Eva admitted.

Eva climbed up behind Tania onto the darkened stage. *Just tell her and get it over with,* she thought.

She took a deep breath.

But before she could say anything, a shadow caught her eye.

A moving shadow.

Eva gasped as a figure rushed from the darkness.

"I'm going to kill you, Tania!" a voice cried. "I'm going to kill you!"

9

*T*ania screamed and jumped away.

She collided with Eva. The two of them staggered backward, then crashed to the floor of the stage.

In a panic, Eva rolled out from under Tania, then scrambled to her feet. As she reached down to pull Tania up, the stage lights burst on.

Eva gasped and shaded her eyes, blinded by the bright overhead spotlights.

"You get everything you want—don't you, Tania?" a voice demanded angrily.

Eva lowered her hand, blinking in the light.

Leslie stood a couple of feet away, glaring furiously at Tania.

"Leslie?" Tania's voice shook. "What . . . what's . . ."

"Yeah, what's going on?" Eva cried. "You scared

us to death! What's the matter with you, anyway?"

"Just stay out of it, Eva," Leslie snapped. "This is between me and Tania."

"What is?" Tania asked. "Leslie, what did I do?"

"Oh, sure," Leslie said sarcastically. "Like you don't know."

"I don't!" Tania cried. "I don't have any idea what you're talking about!"

"Ha." Leslie bared her teeth in a vicious smile. "First you get to be homecoming queen. Now you steal the role in Keith's video. You knew I was counting on that role for my college portfolio! I can't believe you stole that from me too!"

"But—"

"I could *kill* you, Tania!" Leslie clenched her fists. "I really could!"

Eva shuddered. *Leslie is totally out of control,* she realized.

"You don't care about acting," Leslie accused, glaring at Tania. "But I've wanted to act since I was a little girl. And you know it! You know it, and you still took the part from me!"

"Stop it, Leslie!" Tania shouted. "Just stop a second and listen to me!"

"Why should I?"

"Because I didn't even know you wanted to be in the video," Tania explained.

Leslie tossed her head, looking skeptical.

"I *didn't* know," Tania repeated slowly. "Keith never told me. Leslie, I don't blame you for being upset. If Keith had said something, I would have told him to use you. But he didn't!"

Leslie stared at her a moment. Then her shoulders sagged, and the fury went out of her eyes.

Eva sighed in relief.

"I'm really sorry," Tania murmured.

Leslie nodded. "Well . . ." She paused. "I have something to tell *you*, Tania."

"You do?"

"After all, why shouldn't I ruin your day too?" Leslie said bitterly.

"Huh?" Tania frowned. "What do you mean?"

Eva's heart sped up. *Leslie is going to tell her about Sandy and Cherise,* she realized. *I can't let Leslie do it! She'll enjoy it too much. And Tania will be really embarrassed—in front of her biggest rival!*

"What is it?" Tania asked Leslie.

"Not now!" Eva cried. "Leslie, come here."

She grabbed hold of Leslie's arm and pulled her into the wings.

"What is your problem?" Leslie demanded, annoyed.

"I know what you were about to say!" Eva whispered furiously. She squeezed Leslie's arm.

"Don't you *dare* tell her about Sandy! I know you'd just love to hurt her. But don't you dare!"

"Stop it!" Leslie hissed, jerking her arm away.

"*You* stop it!" Eva insisted. "Keep your mouth shut about Sandy and Cherise!"

Leslie glared at her for a moment. Eva stood her ground. "Fine. I won't tell her . . . now," Leslie finally answered.

She spun around and stalked off.

"What was that all about?" Tania asked. "What did she want to tell me?"

Eva took a deep breath.

But as she started to speak, the stage doors clanged open and the rest of the homecoming court trooped in.

I can't tell her now, Eva thought. *Not with people around.* "Nothing," she said, forcing a smile. "Forget it. It wasn't important."

The next afternoon, Eva stood by the big fountain in the mall and gazed around. She and Tania had made plans to meet here to shop for homecoming dresses again. But so far, Eva hadn't spotted her friend.

Of course, it's Saturday, she reminded herself. *The place is packed. Tania's probably stuck in the crowd, trying to find me.*

Eva craned her neck, but it was impossible to see over the heads of all the shoppers. Frustrated, she climbed up onto the low stone wall surrounding the fountain to get a better look.

As she peered around, she spotted a tall guy with curly, reddish-brown hair and a scattering of freckles across his cheeks.

"Jeremy!" Eva stood on tiptoe and waved her arms. "Jeremy!"

Jeremy turned, startled. When he saw Eva, a shy smile spread across his face, and the dimple appeared next to his mouth.

He's so cute, Eva thought. She hopped down from the wall and threaded her way to his side.

"Hey, Eva. I'm glad you saw me," Jeremy said. "I was about to give up trying to find you."

Eva's heart did a little flip. "You were looking for me?"

He nodded. "Tania told me to tell you she'll be late," he explained. "She dropped me off here, but she had to go back home. She has to return something, and she forgot to bring it. She said if you don't want to wait at the fountain, she'd meet you at Pete's Pizza."

"Oh." *Okay, so he was only looking for me so he could deliver a message,* Eva thought. *He's here, isn't he? I should take what I can get.*

"Well, I don't feel like standing around in the crowd," she declared. "Want to get a Coke with me at Pete's?"

"Sure, Eva."

"Great."

Eva took his hand. She began pulling him through the mass of shoppers. *It was a good excuse to hold hands,* she thought.

They got lucky at Pete's and slid into a booth just as another couple was leaving. They ordered their Cokes. Then Eva shrugged out of her jacket and leaned her elbows on the table. She felt almost as if she and Jeremy were really a couple.

"Did you come shopping for something to wear to homecoming too?" she asked. Maybe she could find out if he had a date.

Jeremy shook his head. "I want to check out the home stores," he told her. "My mom's birthday is in a couple of weeks. I thought I'd see if I could find anything." He paused and shook his head again. "I can't believe I said that!"

"What? What's so weird about buying your mother a birthday present?"

"Nothing, except I've never said those words before—'my *mom*,'" he explained. He paused as the waiter set down their Cokes. "It's still new," he added. "Having a family, I mean. Chores and curfews and stuff like that. It's changed my life."

Eva stuck a straw into her soda and laughed. "Wait until you get grounded."

Jeremy's brown eyes turned serious. "I wasn't complaining," he said. "It's great for me. Before Dad married Tania's mom, I was on my own a lot. And I . . . well, I got into some trouble at my old school."

Eva gazed at him curiously. "What kind of trouble?"

"Oh . . ." Jeremy hesitated again. "Never mind. It's in the past. Done. Finished." He quickly gulped some Coke. "Let's not talk about it."

"Sure. Okay." Eva still felt curious, but she didn't push it.

Don't be nosy, she told herself. *He's so quiet. So shy. He probably cut some classes or something. He couldn't possibly have been in any major trouble.*

"Anyway," Jeremy went on. "Having a family is great. Except that Tania's driving everybody nuts about what to wear to the Homecoming Dance. I hope you two find something today—I'm sick of talking about dresses!"

"I hope so," Eva replied. Then, before she lost her nerve, she blurted out, "Speaking of homecoming, do you have a date?"

Jeremy didn't answer. He stared past her, his eyes narrowed.

Great, Eva thought. *He knows I'm going to ask him to go with me. He's trying to figure out how to say no.*

But Jeremy didn't appear to be thinking of an excuse, she realized.

He looked angry. His hand clutched the soda glass tightly. His lips pressed together in a thin line as he kept staring over her shoulder.

Eva turned around.

Sandy and Cherise sat in a booth at the back of the restaurant. They sat on the same side of the table, so close together that Cherise was practically in Sandy's lap.

Disgusted, Eva watched as Sandy pulled Cherise even closer and kissed her on the mouth.

No wonder Jeremy is upset, Eva thought. *Tania is his stepsister. He loves her. And there's her boyfriend, kissing another girl.*

Sandy and Cherise were still locked in a kiss when Eva turned away.

As she did, the door of Pete's Pizza swung open, and a slender girl with blond hair and bright green eyes entered the restaurant.

Tania.

10

*E*va gasped. Would Tania see Sandy and Cherise?

Tania stepped inside the door. A group of kids pushed past her.

Tania shuffled aside to let them pass. She still hadn't looked into the restaurant.

What can I do? Eva wondered frantically. *Go shove Sandy and Cherise under their table? Scream "fire"? Toss my jacket over Tania's head?*

As Eva sat frozen, she heard Jeremy's voice. "I'll get her out of here, Eva. Meet us out by the fountain."

Quickly Jeremy slid out of the booth and hurried over to Tania. Eva watched as he said something to her, then pulled open the door and guided her outside.

Eva let her breath out. *It could have turned*

into a major scene, she thought. *Thank goodness for Jeremy.* As she gathered up her jacket, she glanced toward the back booth.

Sandy and Cherise snuggled close together, nuzzling each other. An untouched pizza sat on the table in front of them.

I hope they get food poisoning or something, Eva thought angrily. *Tania needs to know the truth about what a creep Sandy is.*

Of course, the way Sandy and Cherise are parading around, it's not going to be a secret much longer. Tania is going to find out. And it will be horrible if she finds out by actually seeing them like this.

Making out together as if nobody else existed.

Eva sighed as she put some money on the table and slid out of the booth. *I should have told her yesterday. I'm Tania's best friend. I can't let her go on thinking Sandy cares about her.*

I have to tell her. As soon as I can.

"Hold it, everybody!" Keith cried. "Take a break."

Eva plopped down on the grass and watched as Keith argued with his little sister, Mandy. She had come to the taping, and she was driving Keith nuts.

Finally Keith yelled at Mandy to go wait in the van. She trudged off unhappily.

Eva sighed. It was Monday afternoon, and she

had a ton of homework. The way things were going with the video, she'd be lucky to get home before dinner.

At least Jeremy had come to the shoot today, to give Keith a hand. Maybe she'd get a chance to ask him to the dance. She watched Jeremy and Keith fiddle with the camera. Then she glanced over at Tania.

Tania sat with Sandy, laughing at something he said.

The jerk, Eva thought. She stretched out on her back and stared at the sky. Clouds had blown in. Dark ones, she realized. *If we don't hurry, it's going to rain.*

Eva shivered. She'd been all ready to tell Tania about Sandy on Saturday, after she left Pete's Pizza. But Tania had been so happy, so excited about trying to find the perfect dress for the Homecoming Dance. Eva didn't have the heart to spoil things.

She'd called Tania's house yesterday, but nobody was home.

So here we are again, she thought glumly. Rehearsing the big fight scene between the homecoming queen and her boyfriend.

If Tania only knew how true the scene really is!

Footsteps crunched in the dry grass near Eva's head. She opened her eyes, hoping it was Jeremy.

Sandy stood over her. "What's your problem, Eva?" he asked. "You bored?"

Eva climbed to her feet. "I'm not bored. It's a very interesting scene."

"Yeah," he agreed. "Hey, how do you like the way I play it? I mean, you have to stand there and watch the whole thing. I'm pretty real—right?"

Eva rolled her eyes. "You're totally *unreal*, Sandy."

"Huh?" Sandy scowled at her, insulted. "Well, sorry. Since when did you become a movie critic? Keith thinks I'm okay."

"I'm not talking about the scene, Sandy," Eva told him. "I'm talking about real life."

Sandy put his hands on his hips. "What's that supposed to mean?"

Eva glanced quickly at Tania, who was talking to Keith and Jeremy. She turned back to Sandy. "I know what you're doing," she declared. "I saw you in the gym on Thursday with Cherise. And Saturday I saw the two of you at Pete's. Did you ever get around to eating that pizza, Sandy?"

Sandy stared at her for a moment. But he didn't even appear embarrassed, she noticed. "Hey, I can explain that," he told her. "It's no big deal."

"Really? Try telling that to Tania," Eva snapped. She started to turn away.

"Hey." Sandy caught her by the arm. "You're not going to tell her, are you?"

"What do you care?" Eva asked. "I mean, if you cared, you wouldn't be fooling around with Cherise."

"I told you—I can explain that," Sandy insisted.

Eva yanked her arm free and walked away, disgusted. She heard Sandy following her. But before she could tell him to get lost, Keith called out that he was ready to shoot again.

Eva took her place behind the bleachers and pretended to be frozen in horror as Sandy and Tania began their argument again.

Well, I don't have to pretend, Eva thought. *I am* horrified. *How can Sandy act so casual about cheating on Tania? He actually* said it's no big deal!

"I'm telling you—it's a lie!" Sandy shouted at Tania. They were almost at the end of the scene now.

"Give it a rest!" Tania shouted back. "Everyone in school knows the truth about you!"

Not everyone, Eva thought. *Tania doesn't know. What will she do when I tell her? Will she scream at him like this? Probably not. When Tania gets angry, she goes all cold. She'll probably shut him out.*

Eva's mind snapped back to the scene. It was almost time for her line. Keith would kill her if she messed it up.

Sandy grabbed Tania's arm.

"Stop it!" Eva cried.

Sandy and Tania struggled and fought. Then Sandy began strangling her. Eva yelled again, then hurried toward them. Tania made horrible choking sounds. Sandy's fingers squeezed her neck, tighter and tighter.

Eva filled her lungs so she could do her scream.

"Stop!" Keith suddenly shrieked, startling everyone. *Stop it!*

11

"Stop!" Keith cried again.

Sandy dropped his hands. Tania staggered backward. Eva turned to Keith, wondering what had gone wrong.

"What is it *this* time?" Sandy demanded.

"The camera," Jeremy told him. "It erased all of the data again."

As Sandy stomped away in frustration, Jeremy glared at him. "That's right, Sandy," he called out. "Throw a tantrum. That will really help."

"Jeremy!" Tania stared at him in surprise. "What's *your* problem?"

"Nothing," Jeremy muttered. "Just tired, I guess." He shrugged and turned back to help Keith.

Eva felt surprised too. Jeremy wouldn't usually say anything so sarcastic. *It's because of Tania,* she decided. *Jeremy is as angry at Sandy as I am.*

Sandy stared at Jeremy for a few seconds. Then he hurried over to Tania and flung an arm around her. Tania smiled and leaned her head on his shoulder.

Eva turned away. *Tania likes him so much,* she thought. *She's going to be so upset when I tell her about Cherise.*

"Okay, I reset it, and I think we've got it now," Keith announced. "Let's . . ." He stared up at the sky. "No, wait, this is crazy. It's going to rain any second."

"You mean we're finished for today?" Sandy asked.

"No way. We have to get a good take of this scene." Keith pointed toward the covered bleachers. "We'll shoot there. Come on. Let's do it."

Eva gathered up her backpack and walked with the others to the covered bleachers. Keith showed everybody where to stand. Then he and Jeremy spent a few minutes figuring out camera angles. By the time they were ready, the rain had started.

Eva stood in the aisle between the bleacher seats. Sandy and Tania faced each other on the bottom step of the bleachers. Behind them, Eva could see the rain drizzling from the gray sky.

"Okay, everybody!" Keith called. "And . . . rolling!"

Eva held her breath and watched as Sandy and Tania began to argue. When the time came, she shouted her line.

Tania began making her awful gurgling noises. Her arms dropped to her sides.

Sandy kept squeezing, tighter and tighter.

Tania slumped lifelessly to the ground.

"Keith!" a voice suddenly called out. "Keith, where are you?"

"Cut! Who said that?" Keith demanded.

Eva turned around and saw Keith's little sister trotting up the bleacher steps.

"Mandy!" Keith glared at her. "I told you to wait in the van!"

"I've *been* waiting in the van!" she complained. "It's four thirty. You have to take me to gymnastics, remember?"

Keith yanked at his hair in frustration. "I don't believe this," he muttered. "I do not believe this!"

While Keith argued with his sister, Eva took a deep breath. Her hand stung. Glancing down, she saw that she had scraped it on the cement bleacher wall. A thin line of bright red blood oozed from one of the scratches.

As she fished in her pocket for a tissue, she saw Keith's sister stomp away. Then she noticed Jeremy approaching her.

"You hurt yourself?" Jeremy asked. He took her hand. "I think Keith has a first-aid kit in the van. Want me to get you a . . ." He broke off, staring down the steps.

Eva followed his gaze.

Tania lay still in front of the first row of bleachers.

"Get up, Tania!" Sandy urged, bending over her. "Tania? Hey! Somebody get a bottle of juice!"

"I think I have one," Eva said. "Poor Tania. She really hates this blood sugar problem."

"No! Tania!" Sandy's voice suddenly filled with horror. "No!"

Eva froze as Sandy turned to them, panic in his eyes. "She's not breathing!"

"Huh?" Eva cried out, and grasped the railing.

"What are you *talking* about?" Jeremy demanded. "Check her pulse!"

"I did—I can't find one!" Sandy shrieked. "She's not breathing. She's *dead*!"

He swallowed hard. His eyes locked on Eva's. "But I didn't do it! I didn't!" he cried.

12

With a hoarse cry, Jeremy leaped down the steps. He shoved Sandy roughly aside. Then he dropped to his knees next to Tania.

Eva raced down the steps, trying not to panic. *Tania fainted again, that's all,* she told herself. *Sandy is just putting on another big act to show how much he cares.*

Nothing is wrong. Tania will be fine.

"Nooo!" Jeremy suddenly screamed. "Tania! Tania!"

Eva's heart dropped. *It can't be true,* she thought. *Tania fainted! She can't be . . .*

"She *is* dead!" Jeremy cried. "Tania! Nooo!" He grabbed his stepsister by the shoulders and raised her partway up. "Tania!"

Eva jumped off the last step, almost colliding with Keith. "This can't be real!" Keith said. He turned to Sandy. "What happened?" he demanded.

Sandy frantically shook his head. "Nothing! Nothing happened! She was fine!"

He grabbed Eva, panic in his eyes. "I didn't do it!" he shouted at her. "I didn't!"

As Eva struggled to get away from Sandy, she caught a glimpse of Tania's face.

Her skin was pasty white. Her mouth hung open, and her head flopped limply back.

She's not *breathing,* Eva thought in horror. *It's true! She's dead.*

But how could it happen?

It wasn't the low blood sugar. All that does is make her faint. It couldn't kill her.

How did she die?

A hard, painful lump rose in Eva's throat. Tears spilled from her eyes and rolled down her face. She began to sob.

"Come on, Tania!" Jeremy grabbed Tania's shoulders and frantically began to shake her. "Wake up! You can do it. Come on, Tania!"

Tania's head rolled on her shoulders. Her mouth opened wider, as if she were screaming. But no sound escaped.

"Tania, come *on!*" Jeremy wailed. He shook her harder. "Come on, wake up!"

"Jeremy, stop!" Still sobbing, Eva broke away

from Sandy and gripped Jeremy's arm. "Please, stop it!"

With a cry, Jeremy shrugged Eva off. Eva stumbled backward and bumped into Keith again. "Call an ambulance!" she shouted. "And the police!"

Keith didn't move. He stared at Tania's lifeless body with a dazed expression on his face.

"Please, Keith!" Eva cried. She gave him a little shove. "We need help!"

Keith dragged his gaze away from Tania and blinked at Eva.

"Go on!" she shouted. "Call the police and an ambulance! Find a teacher!"

"Right." Keith spun around, pulling his cell phone out of his pocket as he raced to get help.

"I don't get it!" Sandy muttered to Eva in a panicked voice. "Everything was okay. Really! I just don't *get* what happened!"

Eva stared at him. He had pretended to strangle Tania for the video, she recalled. *Did he get carried away? Did he actually kill her?*

"Why don't you go with Keith?" Eva told him coldly.

"But I want to stay with Tania!"

"What for?" she demanded. "What good can you do now?"

Sandy stared at her for a second. Then he turned and ran off.

Eva swiped the tears from her face and took hold of Jeremy's shoulders. She couldn't bear to look at Tania's face again. "Jeremy," she said softly, "please stop shaking her. Keith went to get help. They'll take care of her. Please."

Jeremy didn't reply. But he finally let go of Tania and set her down gently.

The tears ran across Eva's lips and dripped off her chin. She took a shuddering breath and tried to urge Jeremy to his feet. "Come on. Let's sit down and—"

"No!" Throwing her hands off, Jeremy leaped to his feet. His eyes were wild. "I can't sit here and wait! I have to do *something*!"

Eva reached for him, but Jeremy brushed past her and sprinted away.

"Jeremy!" Eva chased after him, worried. *He's hysterical,* she realized. *He's totally out of his mind. Who knows what he might do?*

"Jeremy!" she called again.

The rain came harder now, soaking her hair and her sweater and mixing with the tears on her face. Out of the corner of her eye, she saw Keith's little sister heading for the bleachers.

"Where's Keith?" Mandy demanded. "What's going on?"

"Get back in the van and wait!" Eva shouted sharply. "Don't move an inch until Keith comes to get you!"

Mandy's eyes grew wide in surprise at Eva's tone of voice. She turned and quickly sprinted away.

Eva kept running, trying to catch up to Jeremy. But his long legs had already carried him across the football field. Eva saw him dart behind the bleachers on the other side and disappear from sight.

Panting, she splashed across the soggy grass and up a little incline. She suddenly heard the wail of sirens.

Eva stopped. *The ambulance and the police,* she thought. *I have to go back. I have to be there when they take Tania away.*

Wiping her eyes again, Eva turned and started back across the football field. As she did, she spotted Keith and Sandy hurrying toward the bleachers from the parking lot at the back of the school. There was no teacher in sight, but at least help was coming.

She glanced over her shoulder. Jeremy trudged slowly toward her from behind the far bleachers. He must have heard the sirens too, Eva realized.

Jeremy kept his head down and his hands jammed into his jeans pockets. Rain dripped from

his hair and soaked his sweatshirt. But he didn't
seem to notice.

Eva stopped and waited for him. Together
they crossed the field to where Tania had fallen,
and Eva stared in shock.

Empty.

"Her bo-body—" Eva stammered. "It's *gone*!"

13

*H*uh? That's impossible!" Jeremy choked out. "Where—where is she?"

Keith shook his head, but didn't speak. Sandy didn't speak either. He gaped at the spot where Tania had been lying, a shocked expression on his face.

Feeling dizzy, Eva closed her eyes. *This* is *impossible*, she thought. *Somebody must have moved Tania. But who?*

"Where is Tania's body?" Jeremy repeated.

"I—I don't know," Keith stuttered. "I . . . She was lying there when I left. I just got back! How should I know what happened?"

Hearing footsteps behind her, Eva opened her eyes and turned around.

Two police officers strode toward them, tense expressions on their faces.

"We got a call about an accidental death," the policewoman said grimly. "The ambulance is on its way." She peered around. "You want to show us the body?"

Eva swallowed. "We can't," she murmured, her voice shaking. "It's . . . I mean, *she's* not here."

The second officer frowned. "Maybe you'd better explain that," he told her.

"We can't," Eva repeated.

The policeman's frown deepened. "Is this some kind of prank?"

"No!" Eva exclaimed. "How can you say that? Tania is dead!" She pointed. "We set her down. Right there. Then Keith went to call you, and Sandy went with him. Jeremy ran off, and I—"

"Whoa, slow down," the woman officer said. Turning to her partner, she told him to call off the ambulance, then go have a look around.

The officer began walking away from the bleachers, using his cell phone to make the call.

Sandy and Jeremy followed him. Down on the field, the three of them went in different directions, searching for Tania's body.

The first officer turned back to Eva and Keith. "Tell me what happened," she ordered. "But start at the beginning."

Keith cleared his throat and began to talk

about the video. Eva barely listened. Tears kept flooding her eyes as she remembered how pale Tania had looked. How her blond hair flew back and forth when Jeremy shook her.

She's dead, Eva told herself. *And now her body's gone. We left her lying here alone, and now she's disappeared!*

Eva took a deep breath and wiped her face. As she did, she glanced up.

Leslie stood at the top of the bleachers, gazing down. The wind swept her long hair back from her face, and Eva could clearly see her expression.

Leslie was smiling.

A chill ran up Eva's spine. The chill she always felt when she sensed that something was wrong.

Does Leslie know something? she wondered.

"Look!" Eva cried, interrupting Keith's story. She pointed up at Leslie. "If you want to know what happened to Tania, try asking her!"

As the policewoman glanced up, Leslie began to edge down the row of seats.

"Hey!" the officer called.

Leslie spun and ran toward the end of the bleachers, her shoes slapping loudly on the concrete.

"Stop her!" the officer shouted.

14

The officer ran off, leaped to the ground, and sprinted around behind the bleachers. Eva could hear her calling to her partner as she ran.

"What was Leslie doing up there?" Keith asked. "Do you think she—"

"I don't know *what* I think." Eva felt herself shaking so hard, her teeth chattered. She stumbled toward the bleachers and sat down. "Leslie had a look on her face. Such a weird smile."

The police officers returned. Leslie walked between them, looking very frightened. Jeremy came up behind them, a confused expression on his face.

"We need you to tell us what you saw," the policewoman said to Leslie.

"I didn't see *any*thing!" Leslie declared.

"Then why did you run?" the policeman asked.

"Because I was scared," Leslie explained. "I mean, I'm just standing up there, right? Then all of a sudden Eva is pointing at me. And two cops start chasing me like I'm some kind of criminal!"

"What were you doing up there?" Eva asked.

"I wanted to see how the video was going. Okay?" Leslie's face flushed. "I couldn't help it. I know I'm not in it, but I couldn't stay away." She shrugged. "When I got here, all I saw was a bunch of people running around in a panic."

"Do you know what happened to Tania's body?" the policewoman asked.

"I told you, I . . ." Leslie broke off, her eyes wide in surprise. "What?" she gasped. "Tania's *body*? What are you *talking* about?"

"Tania is dead," Eva told her. Her voice breaking, she described what had occurred. "Are you sure you didn't see what happened to her, Leslie?"

Stunned, Leslie shook her head. "I told you, I saw everybody running around. I never saw Tania."

Is Leslie telling the truth? Eva wondered. *She seems totally shocked about Tania. But after all, she* does *want to be an actress.*

As the police began asking more questions, Eva started to shiver. The rain had picked up, and so had the wind.

But it's not the weather, Eva thought.

Something's wrong, I can feel it.

She glanced around at the group. Leslie still seemed shocked. So did Keith. Jeremy stared at the ground, a dazed expression on his face.

Everybody's having the right reaction, Eva thought.

But someone is faking.

Someone here is lying.

Eva shivered again. Her weird feelings usually just told her when something wasn't right.

This time, it told her that someone was lying.

But who? she wondered, glancing around again. *Who is it? And what are they lying about?*

Footsteps pounded loudly on the concrete. Sandy suddenly appeared. Rain plastered his light-brown hair to his head, and he gasped for breath.

"Where have *you* been?" Jeremy demanded.

"Looking . . ." Sandy bent over and gulped in some air. "Looking for Tania." He took some more deep breaths, then straightened up and slicked the rain out of his hair. "I thought she'd be waiting in my car, but . . ."

Jeremy's head snapped up. "What did you say?"

"How could she be waiting in your car?" Keith asked. "She's dead, remember?"

Sandy glanced away, looking uncomfortable.

Jeremy stepped toward him. "You know something, Sandy! What is it? What are you hiding?"

"If you know something, you'd better tell us," the policewoman warned. "I don't need to tell you this is serious. You could get in a lot of trouble if you don't tell us everything."

"Okay, okay, I'll tell you!" Sandy wiped rainwater from his hair again. "Look, this wasn't supposed to happen, okay?"

"*What* wasn't?" Jeremy demanded. "What are you talking about?"

"It started out as a joke. Tania and I cooked it up," Sandy explained. "The idea was, I'd strangle her for the movie. She'd pretend to be dead, and I'd go along with it. We just wanted to shake everyone up. For fun."

"Huh?" Eva let out a shocked cry.

"You and Tania decided to play games with my movie?" Keith cried.

"Yeah, for fun," Sandy repeated.

Eva gaped at him. "That's a terrible joke," she declared. "How could you and Tania do something so awful?"

"Never mind that. Where is she?" Jeremy asked. "Where is Tania?"

"That's the problem," Sandy told him. "See,

after everybody got all crazy, Tania was supposed to jump up and yell 'Surprise!'"

"But she didn't," Eva reminded him. "And besides, Jeremy ran down and grabbed her. He would have known if she was faking!"

Jeremy shook his head. "I was too freaked to really check her," he said. "She was so still!"

"Right—and that was part of the plan," Sandy explained. "I figured she was really into the joke, you know? I mean, she wasn't going to jump up until everybody started running around like crazy anyway."

Jeremy glared at him. "So when did you decide this wasn't such a great joke?"

"When Tania disappeared. That wasn't part of the plan." Sandy gazed around as if he were looking for Tania to suddenly reappear. "But she really is gone! I don't know where she is!"

Eva stared at Sandy. *Is he lying? I can't tell. He looks confused and worried, but so does everybody else. Someone is faking, but who?*

And what happened to Tania? Did she really die?

"Go back a couple of steps," the policewoman told Sandy. "This strangling scene for the video— you and Tania both decided to *pretend* you'd really killed her?"

Sandy nodded. "She'd act dead. Then I'd check

her and start screaming. We just wanted to freak everyone out. But—"

"Okay, so you checked her," the officer said. "Was she breathing then?"

"Yes." Sandy paused, frowning. "Well . . ."

"Well, what?" Jeremy demanded. "Was she breathing or not?"

"I *think* she was," Sandy replied shakily.

"How could you not know?" Jeremy wailed.

"Because I was only pretending and I didn't check very carefully." Sandy closed his eyes. "I thought she was breathing, but . . . but now I'm not sure."

"You did it!" Jeremy accused.

Sandy's eyes snapped open.

"You did it!" Jeremy repeated. "You strangled her! You killed my sister!"

Stunned, Sandy backed away.

Jeremy leaped at him and pounded him with his fists. "You killed Tania!" he screamed in a fury. "You strangled her! Then your *other* girlfriend came and got rid of the body, right?"

"My other . . . ," Sandy started to say.

But the words choked in his throat as Jeremy's hands clamped tightly around his neck and began to strangle him.

15

"hoa! Back off—now!" the policewoman shouted. She and her partner grabbed Jeremy and pulled him off Sandy. "Ease up!"

"Let me go!" Jeremy cried. "He killed her. He killed Tania!"

"Jeremy, stop!" Eva begged. "Please!"

Keith and Leslie shouted at him too, but Jeremy ignored everyone.

He's so furious, he wants to kill Sandy, Eva thought in horror. *But it won't help Tania. It won't help anything!*

Finally the police wrestled Jeremy over to one of the bleacher seats.

Sandy staggered backward, holding his throat and gasping.

"Sandy!" Leslie cried. "Are you all right?" She ran to him and put her arms around him, holding him close. "Can you breathe okay? Can you talk?"

Sandy cleared his throat. "I'm okay," he rasped.

Eva glanced at Jeremy. He had stopped resisting the police. But he stood tensely, breathing hard, clenching and unclenching his hands.

"Jeremy, we understand you're upset," the policeman told him. "But you have to get ahold of yourself and listen." He put his hand on Jeremy's shoulder and pushed firmly.

Jeremy sat down, still looking tense.

"We think your sister walked away," the officer declared. "We don't think she's dead."

"What?" Jeremy shook his head. "I don't believe it. You didn't see her lying there. Besides, didn't you hear what Sandy said? He isn't sure if she was breathing!"

"We heard it all," the policewoman assured him. "Now listen—bodies don't just disappear. This whole thing started out as a joke, remember?"

Jeremy nodded.

"And that's probably what this disappearance is," the policewoman went on. "Some kind of joke."

"But what if it's not?" Keith asked.

"If it's not, we'll get to the bottom of it," the policewoman assured him. "But we think it is."

Can she be right? Eva wondered.

The policewoman patted Jeremy's back. "When

a prank gets out of hand like this, people get upset," she told him. "The important thing is for everyone to stay calm."

Eva raised her eyes to look at Sandy. He stood with Leslie. She had her arm through his and was murmuring softly to him. But Sandy didn't seem to notice. He kept rubbing his throat, a stunned expression in his eyes.

Eva walked over to Jeremy. He sat with his shoulders slumped, staring at his feet.

Poor Jeremy, Eva thought. *He was so happy a couple of days ago, talking about how he finally got a family.*

And now he may have lost Tania.

Eva took Jeremy's hand and gave it a squeeze.

"All right, I think we're finished here," the policewoman announced. She patted Jeremy on the back again. "Why don't we give you a ride home?" she suggested. "Your sister is probably there right now, enjoying a good laugh."

Can that be true? Eva wondered again as she and Jeremy stood up. *Is Tania really okay?*

Fifteen minutes later, the police car dropped Eva off at her house. Eva thanked the driver, then raced up the walk and hurried inside.

No one home.

Eva dropped her book bag onto the floor and pulled off her muddy sneakers. Then she crossed the hall and ran upstairs to her bedroom.

The police had dropped her off before taking Jeremy home. She was desperate to call the Darmans' house and see if Tania really was there.

Wouldn't it be great if Tania is at home, laughing it up? she thought as she snatched up her phone. *Of course, I'll be totally furious with her. But I'll be so happy.*

Eva quickly called her and waited.

Straight to voicemail.

Eva ended the call, then tried again.

Still straight to voicemail.

What does that mean? she wondered. *Is Tania trying to call me to let me know she's okay?*

Hoping the phone would ring if she left it alone, Eva changed into dry jeans and a thick cotton sweater.

The phone stayed silent.

She brushed out her dark hair, then twisted it into a single braid that hung down her back.

Still no call from Tania.

Frustrated and impatient, she grabbed the phone and dialed again. No luck.

What's going on? What went on? Did Tania play a joke, or did she really disappear?

Did she really die?

As Eva paced her bedroom, she pictured Tania lying so still in front of the camera.

"The camera!" Eva gasped. *Maybe it stayed on the whole time. Keith left it on the tripod when we all ran off. Did he leave it running?*

If he did, the whole thing would be on the video. We might be able to see what happened to Tania's body!

Eva grabbed her phone again and called Keith. He picked up on the first ring. "Jeremy?" he asked eagerly.

"No, it's Eva," she told him. "I haven't heard from Jeremy either. Or Tania. But listen, I had an idea. You know when you went to get help, and I went running after Jeremy? Did you leave the camera on?"

"Hey, I had the exact same idea!" Keith cried. "I was just about to check the video. Why don't you come over? I'll wait and we can watch it together."

Eva hung up and raced downstairs. *Please let the video show something,* she thought as she drove to Keith's. *Let it show Tania hopping to her feet and making a funny face at the camera.*

Or someone coming and taking Tania's body away.

Anything! As long as we can find out what happened to her.

She pulled into Keith's driveway, and saw him standing in the open front door, waiting for her. She slammed the car door and hurried up to the house.

"Let's take a look," Keith said. He turned and led her down the hall into a small room filled with metal shelves holding video equipment.

An overstuffed couch covered with throw pillows stood in the middle of the room. Across from it was a huge television monitor.

Eva sat down while Keith cued up the video. He pressed play, then joined her on the couch.

"Here goes," he murmured.

Eva leaned forward tensely, eyes glued to the monitor.

What will it show? she wondered.

What happened to Tania?

16

A black, blank image filled the television screen.

"What's wrong?" Eva asked.

"Nothing. It'll play in a second," Keith assured her. "I *think*."

They sat, watching the blank screen. "Come on!" Keith urged. "Come on!"

Nothing happened.

"Fast-forward it," Eva told him.

"Yeah. Right." Keith punched the control, but the screen didn't clear. "Great," he muttered, rolling his eyes. "Just great."

"What is it?"

"The camera. It malfunctioned again, and I didn't know it." Keith raked his hair in frustration. "We got nothing!"

Eva sighed in disappointment. "I thought for sure it would tell us what happened."

"Me too." Keith flopped down onto the couch beside her. "What do *you* think, Eva? Where's Tania?"

Eva shook her head. "I just don't know. I hope the police were right about it being a joke. But I have such a bad feeling about this whole thing. Anyway, if it *was* a joke, why hasn't she called me?"

"I'll try her," Keith said. He fumbled under a couch pillow and pulled out his phone.

Eva could hear Tania's voicemail message the second he put the phone up to his ear. "Maybe she's on the phone, talking to someone else. Maybe she's trying to call me."

"I wish." Blushing, Keith put the phone down and stood up. "I mean, I wish she was calling *some-body*, not just me."

Eva smiled. "It's okay, Keith. I know you've got a crush on her."

"Everyone knows," he said. "That's my problem."

"What do you mean?"

"Well, Tania is missing, maybe dead," Keith said. "I'm . . . I was . . . crazy about her, and I feel awful about what happened." He shoved his hands into his pockets. "But I still have a video to do."

"Oh." Eva nodded. "The show must go on, huh? You have to get someone else to play Tania's part."

"I can't help it," he told her. "I feel terrible, but I *have* to finish the video. If I don't, I won't have anything to send to the film schools. It's really important."

"So was Tania," Eva declared.

"I know that!" Keith exclaimed. "That's why I'm so upset."

Before Eva could reply, the door to the room opened and Jeremy burst in.

"Jeremy?" Eva jumped up, her heart pounding. "Where's Tania? Is she okay?"

"Was she at home like the cops thought?" Keith asked.

Jeremy shook his head. "She wasn't there. Her room looks the same as it did this morning. Tania hasn't been home at all!"

Eva's knees shook. She sat down quickly.

Tania is dead, she thought. *She didn't go home. It wasn't a joke.*

She's dead.

"I've been on the phone since I got back. I called everybody I could think of, all the numbers in her contacts." Jeremy paced the room, his brown eyes frantic. "Nobody has seen her. Nobody knows where she is!"

"What about the cops?" Keith asked. "What did they say when they saw she wasn't at home?"

"The cops—ha!" Jeremy slammed a fist into his palm. "They still think the whole thing's a big joke!"

"They *can't*," Eva cried.

"Yeah, well, they do," Jeremy insisted. "Or if it's not a joke, they think she ran away or something."

"Ran away from home?" Eva shook her head. "Tania wouldn't do that."

"That's what I told them," Jeremy agreed. "All they say is 'Sit tight, Jeremy. She'll show up.' Like I can really sit around twiddling my thumbs while my sister's missing!"

Still pacing, Jeremy bumped into one of the metal shelves. The shelf wobbled. A pile of cords slid off and clattered to the floor.

"Hey, careful," Keith warned him, crossing the room to pick up the cords. "Why don't you sit down and try to cool off?"

"You sound like the police," Jeremy snapped. But he helped Keith gather the cords and stack them back on the shelf.

Eva stayed on the couch, staring at the floor. She couldn't stop shivering even though the little room was warm and stuffy.

Something is so wrong. I can feel it.

She wished she could ignore it, but she'd had

these feelings too many times before. She hated them, but she trusted them.

Somebody was lying earlier today, she thought. *That's all I know.*

"Come on, sit down," Keith urged Jeremy after they finished with the cords. "Crashing around the room won't help anything. Let's talk. Maybe we can make some sense out of this whole thing."

Jeremy shook his head. "I don't need to talk. I already know what happened. Sandy is a murderer."

Eva stared at him. *How could he possibly think that?*

"What are you talking about?" Keith asked, shocked. "He's not a murderer. Sure, he can be a pain in the neck. But he's not a killer. I've known him my whole life."

"You're wrong," Jeremy insisted fiercely. "I *know* Sandy really killed Tania. You want to know how, right? Okay, I'll tell you. I'll tell you something I didn't tell the police."

"What?" Eva cried. "What didn't you tell the police?"

17

Jeremy stood in the middle of the room, his brown eyes narrowed in anger. "I overheard Sandy and Cherise planning to kill Tania," he said. "That's how I know that Sandy killed her. I heard him plotting to do it."

Eva gasped.

Keith shook his head. "Are you nuts?" he asked, his voice rising. "Are you totally nuts?"

Maybe that's it, Eva thought. *Not that Jeremy is nuts, but he's too freaked out about Tania to think straight. Why else would he say something like that?*

"You can think I'm crazy," Jeremy said. "I don't care. I know what I heard. It was before the shoot today. I was at my locker, and I heard these two people. They were around the corner from my locker, whispering together. I caught Tania's name, so I sneaked up and listened."

He slammed his fist against the wall. "And I heard everything!"

Keith still looked skeptical. "Why didn't you tell the police?"

"I don't know!" Jeremy cried. "I was out of my head. I couldn't think clearly—about anything!"

But is he really thinking clearly now? Eva wondered.

Keith moved to the couch and picked up his phone. "Then we should call the police now and tell them what you heard."

"No!" Eva pulled the phone from Keith's hand. "You could get Cherise and Sandy into major trouble!"

"Good," Jeremy declared grimly. "They deserve it."

"Not if it's not true," Eva argued. "Look, they were whispering. I'm not saying you made it up, but maybe you didn't hear right."

"No way!" Jeremy insisted bitterly.

"Let me talk to Cherise first," Eva said. "I'll go over and see her. I'm sure it's a misunderstanding. We shouldn't accuse her if it isn't true!"

Jeremy nodded reluctantly.

It can't be true, Eva told herself. *It has to be a horrible mistake!*

Late the next morning, Eva gulped down some orange juice and checked the clock. Almost eleven thirty. With no school because of teacher conferences, she'd overslept. She'd better hurry if she wanted to catch Cherise at home.

There'd been no answer from Cherise last night. Eva had tried calling her after leaving Keith's. But she finally gave up and decided to go over there this morning.

As she drove down Park Drive toward Cherise's house, her hands started to sweat and her heart thudded anxiously. The rain clouds had disappeared and the fall leaves were gorgeous in the sunlight.

But Eva still couldn't shake the strange feeling she'd had since before Tania disappeared. It made the beautiful day seem dark and gloomy.

And now she had to go and tell Cherise that Jeremy thought she was a murderer.

How can I say it? she wondered as she turned onto Cherise's street. *By the way, Cherise, Jeremy heard you and Sandy planning to kill Tania. Is it true?*

Eva sighed. *Maybe that's the only way,* she thought. *Just come right out and tell her.*

Eva slowed the car, peering out the passenger window. Cherise lived in a yellow, two-story house, she remembered. With a wide front porch and an old-fashioned swing that hung on chains from the porch ceiling.

There it was. Eva pulled to the curb and started to shut the engine off. As she did, she glanced up at the house again.

Her hand froze on the key.

Cherise sat on the porch swing, her red hair glowing in the sun.

Sandy sat beside her—close beside her—his arm around her shoulders.

As Eva watched, Cherise leaned even closer to Sandy and kissed him. Then they both stood up.

Eva carefully eased the car into reverse and backed down the street. *It doesn't mean anything,* she told herself. *I already knew Sandy was fooling around with Cherise. Just because they're making out doesn't mean they killed Tania.*

Eva stopped the car and peered out the windshield.

Sandy and Cherise stood near the front steps now, their arms around each other. They kissed again, then broke apart.

Sandy trotted down the porch steps. He turned and gave Cherise a wave, then hurried down the walkway toward the street.

Eva watched as he climbed into his car and pulled away. He drove off in the other direction.

When she glanced at the house again, the porch was empty. Cherise must have gone inside.

Go ahead, Eva told herself. *Just go talk to her. See what she says.* She shut the car off, got out, and walked the half block to Cherise's house.

As she climbed the porch steps, a gust of wind came up. The swing squeaked on its chains, and the screen door rattled noisily. Above the noise, Eva thought she heard another sound.

A voice.

She paused, listening.

Yes. Cherise's voice.

Eva raised her hand to knock on the screen door.

And froze as she heard Cherise's voice again. Louder this time. High-pitched and furious.

"I'll kill you!" Cherise screamed. "I'll kill you, too!"

18

*E*va dropped back, her heart racing.

"I'll kill you, too!" Cherise shrieked. "Don't think I won't!"

Call the police! Eva told herself. *Go next door and get help!* As she turned to run, another gust of wind set the swing in motion, crashing it into her.

She stumbled sideways. As she reached out to grab the porch railing, she heard the screen door rattle behind her.

"Eva?" Cherise called. "Hi. I thought I heard somebody out here."

Eva caught her balance and turned around.

Cherise stood behind her, one arm propping the door open. "You look upset," she said.

"Who was screaming?" Eva demanded. "I heard—"

As Cherise started to reply, another voice

drowned her out. "Go ahead and laugh!" it screamed. "It's the last laugh you'll ever have!"

Cherise glanced behind her, into the house. "Terri, would you turn that down?" she shouted. She turned back to Eva. "My sister," she explained. "She's watching TV. She *always* plays it too loud."

The screaming voice grew softer.

"I thought it was real." Eva laughed. "I guess I'm feeling kind of jumpy."

Cherise pushed the door open wider. "Come on in. Want a Coke?"

Eva nodded and followed her down a hall. They passed the living room where Cherise's sister sat staring at the television, and turned through a door into a big, sunny kitchen.

"Sit down." Cherise pulled two cans of soda from the refrigerator and set them on a round wooden table. "You still look upset," she declared as she took glasses from the counter and filled them with ice. "It's because of Tania, isn't it?"

Eva nodded. She popped the top on her soda and poured some. Her hand shook as she raised the glass. She set it back down.

"Hey, you're really freaked," Cherise commented. "I mean, I don't blame you. Tania's your best friend. You must feel awful. Well, everybody does."

Eva nodded again. *Does Cherise really feel*

awful? she wondered. "It's so horrible," Eva murmured. She managed to pick up the glass without sloshing any soda out.

"Yeah," Cherise agreed. "What do you think happened? I don't mean to sound morbid, but do you think she's dead?"

"I don't know," Eva replied. She wondered if Cherise knew. "I wish I did. Not knowing is the worst."

"That's what Sandy says."

Eva glanced at her. "He does?"

"Sure." Cherise twisted a strand of red hair around her finger, a worried expression on her face. "He's just a total mess because of it."

Eva drank some more Coke. *Go ahead and tell her,* she urged herself. *Tell her what Jeremy said. Get it over with.* She took a deep breath. "Um . . . listen, Cherise. Jeremy heard you and Sandy talking yesterday."

"Oh?" Cherise crunched an ice cube. "What about?"

"Well, that's what I came over here for," Eva explained. "Jeremy thinks he heard you and Sandy plotting to . . . to kill Tania."

Cherise's blue eyes widened in shock. "That's *crazy!*" she cried, jumping up from her chair. "How can you say that?"

"*I* didn't say it," Eva replied. "Jeremy did."

"Well, he's wrong!" Cherise declared. "He's totally wrong! When did he hear us, anyway? Where?"

"At school," Eva explained. "Yesterday afternoon, right before the shoot. He was at his locker and you two were around the corner from him."

Cherise thought about it a moment. "Oh!" she cried. "I know what that was! I was helping Sandy rehearse for Keith's video. I was helping him learn his lines!"

Eva felt a surge of relief. Keith's script was full of lines like the one Jeremy overheard. Cherise's explanation made total sense.

Thank goodness, she thought. *Now I don't have to walk around thinking Cherise is a killer.*

"I can't believe Jeremy would accuse us of something like that!" Cherise declared. "That's horrible!"

"He's kind of a mess too," Eva reminded her.

"Yeah. I guess so." As Cherise started toward the table for her soda, her phone rang. She turned back to the counter, and picked up. "Hello?"

A muffled hissing sound filled the room. Eva glanced around.

"Speakerphone," Cherise whispered to her. "Hello?" she repeated.

The hissing stopped.

Eva heard the caller take a long, slow breath.

And then an eerie, whispery voice filled the kitchen. *"I killed Tania,"* it rasped. *"You're next."*

19

*E*va gasped as the words echoed in the big kitchen.

"Who is this?" Cherise demanded. The blood had drained from her face. "What are you talking about?"

"Tania was first," the voice rasped. "You're next."

Cherise hung up and wrapped her arms around herself with a shiver. "Who *was* that?" she asked shrilly.

Eva shook her head. "I don't know."

Cherise shivered again. "I couldn't even tell who they were talking to! Me? You? Both of us?"

Eva didn't reply. She stared at her glass of soda, trying to figure out what was going on.

"Eva? What are you thinking?" Cherise asked.

"Something is wrong," Eva told her.

"No kidding."

Eva shook her head again. "No, I mean this whole thing just doesn't feel right. Something is not the way it seems."

"Well, what?" Cherise demanded.

"I don't have a clue," Eva admitted. "It's a feeling."

"Oh. One of your psychic ones." Cherise sounded skeptical.

"They've never been wrong," Eva told her. "But it's not like a vision or anything like that. I can just feel when something is wrong."

"Too bad your 'feeling' can't tell us who called." Cherise rubbed her arms and eyed the phone warily. "That voice really spooked me. I keep trying to convince myself it was just a prank call."

"Me too. But we'd better report it to the police." Eva sighed as Cherise picked up the phone. *The caller said they killed Tania,* she thought. *Maybe Tania really is dead.*

"Whoa! That must have freaked you out," Keith declared after school the next day. "What did he say again?"

"He said 'I killed Tania. You're next,'" Eva repeated. "But I couldn't really tell if it was a he— and neither could Cherise. The voice was so weird. Harsh and whispery."

Eva shivered as she stood with Keith in the school parking lot. Dry leaves skittered around in the wind, and dark clouds raced across the sky.

Winter will be here soon, she thought, shivering again.

And Tania is still missing.

She gazed across the parking lot. Jeremy leaned against the side of a car, a glum expression on his face. She'd just told him and Keith about the call.

Jeremy hadn't said a word. He'd just walked halfway across the parking lot and then stopped, as if he couldn't decide what to do or where to go.

The longer Tania stays missing, the more worried he gets, Eva thought. *And telling him about the call didn't help. If only I could figure out what's going on!*

"So what did the police say?" Keith asked, interrupting Eva's thoughts.

"I told you. They didn't believe me." Eva scowled. "They still think the whole thing is a joke."

"Some joke," Keith muttered. "I can't believe they aren't taking it seriously."

Eva nodded. *It doesn't make sense,* she thought.

None of this makes sense.

"Well, listen. I have to go," Keith told her, zipping up his black leather jacket. "Uh-oh," he murmured. "Here comes trouble."

Eva turned and saw Leslie striding toward them, her long brown hair blowing in the wind. "Keith!" Leslie called out. "I need to talk to you!"

Keith sighed.

"What's the problem?" Eva whispered to him.

"She wants to be a star, that's the problem," he murmured. "She won't get out of my face."

Leslie hurried up to them. "I've been trying to call you, Keith," she told him accusingly.

"Yeah. Well, I've been kind of busy."

"And kind of worried," Eva added. "About Tania, remember?"

Leslie scowled, insulted. "Of course I remember." She pulled a strand of hair out of her eyes and turned to Keith again. "That's one of the reasons I want to talk to you."

Keith's eyes lit up. "You know something about her?"

"No. How should I?" Leslie asked impatiently. "Anyway, I know you need someone to play the homecoming queen in your video. So I've decided to forget how you dumped me from the part. I'll do it."

"Um . . ." Keith shifted his weight and glanced around.

"What's the problem?" Leslie asked. "You *do* need an actress, right?"

"Well . . . no. Sorry," Keith told her. "But I've dropped the homecoming queen idea."

Eva stared at him in surprise. He hadn't told her. She knew how much that video meant to him, but she felt glad anyway. With Tania gone, it wouldn't be the same.

"But you have to have *some*thing to show the film schools," Leslie insisted. "You're not giving up, are you?"

"No way," Keith replied. "I'm working on another video now. With Sandy."

"Oh?" Leslie's eyes gleamed with interest. "What's it about? Is there a part for me?"

Keith shook his head. "Sorry," he repeated. "It's kind of a secret project."

Leslie scowled at him. "And you're doing it with Sandy. And there's nothing in it for me."

"Right."

Leslie tossed her hair back and glared at him.

Keith shrugged. "Sorry," he told her for the third time.

"Oh, stop saying that!" Leslie snapped. "You're not sorry at all!"

Keith shrugged again. "Whatever."

Eva turned away, thinking she'd go over and try to cheer Jeremy up.

But Jeremy had left. Instead Eva saw Sandy walking toward them.

Leslie spotted him too. She sucked in her breath and stalked away, giving Sandy a disgusted glance as she passed him.

"What's her problem?" Sandy asked as he shuffled slowly up to them. "Never mind. I don't want to hear it. I was halfway home when I realized I forgot all my books. I must be losing my mind."

Eva stared at him. "You look terrible," she told him.

"I feel terrible." Sandy blinked his red-rimmed eyes. "I haven't slept. I can't. I can't stop thinking about Tania."

"Nobody can," Eva murmured. "We're all worried out of our minds."

"Yeah." Keith punched Sandy lightly on the arm. "Go home, man. At least try to sleep. You look like the walking dead."

Sandy nodded and headed into the school.

"You want a ride home?" Keith asked Eva.

"No, thanks. I think I'll see if Jeremy's still around somewhere." Eva nodded goodbye to Keith, then crossed the parking lot.

She glanced around, thinking Jeremy might have just moved down the row of cars. But she didn't see him. He wasn't on the sidewalk or the hill that led toward the football field either.

He must have gone home, Eva decided. She began to leave the parking lot, then realized she'd forgotten her backpack. *Sandy's not the only one who's too upset to remember things,* she thought.

Eva ran across the windy lot and into the school. As she passed the auditorium, she heard voices coming from inside. Were they practicing for the homecoming ceremony, without Tania?

She couldn't stand to know. She hurried past the doors and trotted up to the second floor. She heard a locker slam somewhere in the distance. Then she heard footsteps echoing loudly in the empty hall.

Rounding the corner, Eva saw Leslie rushing toward her.

She saw Leslie's frightened expression.

Then she saw the dark stain on Leslie's yellow sweater.

"Leslie!" Eva cried. "What is all that blood?"

20

Leslie stopped quickly and flung her hair out of her face.

Eva sucked in her breath, shocked and frightened. She stared hard at Leslie. At the blood-stain on the front of her sweater.

Then she raised her eyes to Leslie's face—and gasped.

A streak of blood washed across one of Leslie's cheeks and dripped slowly down, onto her neck. Beads of bright red glistened on her eyelashes and scattered across her cheeks.

Her hands looked as if she'd dipped them into a bucket of blood.

"Leslie, you're hurt!" Eva cried.

"I'm okay, I think." Leslie raised a bloody hand and pushed her hair away again. "It's kind of embarrassing, actually."

"What are you talking about?"

"I was so furious, Eva, I lost my temper." Leslie's lips quivered. "I just blew up! And I . . . I slammed my locker door against the wall."

"Your locker . . ." Eva's words caught in her throat.

Leslie took a deep breath. "I keep a mirror hanging inside the locker," she explained. Her voice shook, and her gaze kept skipping around the hall. She wiped her hands on her jeans. As she did, she winced. "When I opened the locker, I slammed the door back really hard. The mirror broke. And I cut myself."

"Where?" Eva asked.

"The mirror just shattered!" Leslie cried. "Pieces of glass sprayed all over me." A drop of blood spilled from Leslie's eyelashes and rolled toward her mouth. She wiped it away.

Eva put an arm around her shoulders. "Come on. Let's go into the bathroom. I'll help you clean up."

"I just want to get out of here," Leslie declared.

"You can't walk around with that blood all over you," Eva insisted, pulling her toward the bathroom across the hall. "You'll give people a heart attack. You almost gave me one."

In the bathroom, Leslie leaned against the tile wall and closed her eyes. Eva wadded up a bunch of paper towels and dampened them in cool water. Then she gently wiped Leslie's face and hands and neck, getting as much blood off as she could.

"That's good enough." Leslie pushed herself away from the wall. "Thanks, Eva, but I need to get away from here."

"Want to borrow my jacket to cover up?" Eva asked, tossing the towels into the trash can. "It's in my locker."

Leslie shook her head, her face pale. "No. I just want to go home." She checked herself in the mirror, then pulled open the door. "Thanks for helping, Eva," she called back over her shoulder.

Eva washed her hands and left the bathroom. *All I want to do is go home too,* she thought as she walked down the hall. *Go home, crawl under the covers, and go to sleep. Maybe when I wake up, this awful feeling will be gone.*

But she knew it wouldn't.

Eva turned another corner and hurried toward her locker. As she drew closer, she saw a dark stain on the floor in front of it.

No, not a stain. A dark puddle.

Sidestepping it, Eva spun the combination lock and yanked open the door.

"Huh?" She let out a startled cry as a boy tumbled out of the locker.

Eva stared in horror at the thick, brownish-blond hair and the good-looking face of Sandy Bishop.

Sandy's eyes were closed.

His lips were drawn back from his teeth, as if he were screaming.

His body slid slowly from the locker. His shoulders, his chest, his legs. He twisted as he fell, and then his face slammed into the puddle of blood on the floor.

Blood, Eva thought as her heart thundered loudly. *Sandy's blood!*

She reached toward him, her hand shaking.

Then she saw the knife.

A thick-handled knife, stuck halfway to the hilt in Sandy's back.

Feeling dizzy, Eva jerked her hand away and straight up. As she did, she caught sight of the words on the inside of her locker door.

The words scrawled in blood.

Sandy's blood.

Your Turn Next

Eva's own blood pounded in her ears. She wanted to run, but she couldn't move.

She couldn't take her eyes off Sandy. *Somebody*

killed him, she thought. *Stabbed him in the back.*

And I'm next.

Terrified, she raised her hands to her hair and began to scream.

21

I still can't believe it!" Cherise cried. "Sandy — dead! It's like a nightmare!"

Cherise sat on one end of the couch in Eva's living room. Leslie sat at the other end. Keith paced the floor, stopping every once in a while to glance out the front window. Jeremy sat tensely on the low stone ledge in front of the fireplace, clutching a can of soda and staring at the rug.

Eva sat in a soft, fat armchair and listened as the others discussed Sandy's murder.

I'm so exhausted, she thought. *It must be from the shock.*

It had been three hours since she'd discovered Sandy's body. The police came. And after they talked to Eva, they rounded up Sandy's friends and questioned them. Afterward, they all gathered at Eva's house.

Nobody wants to go home yet, Eva thought, glancing around. *We're all so upset.*

And so frightened.

What is going on?

"I mean, what is going on?" Cherise wailed, echoing Eva's thought. "This is totally unbelievable!"

"You already said that a zillion times," Keith groaned.

"Well, excuse me," Cherise snapped. "I suppose you think it's normal to have dead bodies falling out of lockers!"

Eva shuddered and curled her legs underneath her.

"Sorry, Eva," Cherise said. She sighed and twisted a strand of hair around her finger. "Sorry, everybody. I guess I'm a little freaked."

"We all are." Jeremy's voice sounded hollow.

Keith peered out the window for a moment, then began pacing again. As he did, he held up the fingers of one hand. "Tania's gone." He bent a finger down. "Eva and Cherise get a threatening phone call. Sandy is murdered. And Eva finds a threatening message."

Keith bent the last finger and clenched his fist. "What does it all mean?"

Eva shuddered again, remembering those bloody words.

Your Turn Next.

She knew what *that* meant.

But did someone really plan to kill her?

"I keep trying to figure out what's coming," Keith went on. "You know, like I'm watching a movie or something. Trying to guess what's going to happen."

Jeremy raised his head. "It's not a movie plot, Keith. Unfortunately, it's real."

"Well, it doesn't hurt to try to figure things out," Cherise told him. "Maybe if we do, this awful nightmare will be over." Tears welled up in her eyes, and she plucked a tissue from the box on the end table.

"Somebody's trying to kill us. That's what's happening," Keith declared.

Is that true? Eva wondered. *Tania's missing. And Sandy's dead, and I got that message. But still . . . something doesn't make sense.*

Something feels wrong.

"What I want to know is why someone's doing it," Keith said. "Why would someone want us dead?"

"Who cares why?" Cherise asked. "The important thing is *who!*"

Everyone turned to Leslie.

She sat huddled on the couch, nervously chewing on a thumbnail.

Did Leslie really cut herself on a mirror this afternoon? Eva wondered.

Or did she kill Sandy?

Feeling everyone's eyes on her, Leslie stopped chewing her nail and stared back. "Don't look at me like that," she told them.

Eva dropped her eyes, feeling slightly ashamed. Okay, so Leslie had a bad temper. And she was furious with Tania *and* with Sandy.

That didn't make her a killer, did it?

"The police grilled me too, remember?" Leslie reminded them in a shaky voice. "I was alone in the school. Eva found me covered with blood. They kept asking me what happened, over and over and over! It was horrible. And now you guys are staring at me as if you suspect me too!"

"Look, we're upset and scared," Keith said.

"So am I!" Leslie insisted. "But I'm not a killer. None of us are. We're all just normal kids. Who is doing this?"

Eva's phone rang shrilly, and everyone jumped.

Eva slipped out of the chair. *It's Mom,* she thought as she went to answer. *Probably calling to say she's leaving work now. Thank goodness she wasn't home when we got here.*

She's going to freak when she hears what happened to Sandy.

But it was from a number Eva didn't recognize. Still, Eva answered. "Hello?" she said.

Silence.

And then a low, raspy voice came over the line. The same voice Eva had heard at Cherise's house.

"*Your turn next,*" it whispered.

"What?" Eva gripped the phone so hard, her knuckles turned white. "Who *is* this? What are you trying—"

"Your turn next," the voice interrupted. "First Tania. Then Sandy."

Silence for a second.

Eva waited, her heart pounding.

"Then *you,*" the voice whispered.

22

I really don't feel like doing this," Eva told Keith the next afternoon.

"Come on, Eva." Keith held the camera up and gave her a pleading look. "It won't take long."

Eva yanked her hair out of her face and glanced up at the top of the football stadium bleachers. "I didn't braid my hair. This wind will turn it into a tumbleweed."

Keith rolled his eyes. "Don't worry about the way you look. These are supposed to be candid video portraits of my friends, remember? It's not a modeling job, for crying out loud."

"What am I supposed to do, anyway?"

"Just talk to the camera," Keith told her. He turned and started up the steps. "Or you and Cherise can talk to each other. She's coming too, remember?"

"Well, why do we have to be outside?" Eva asked. "Why can't we go in where it's warm?"

Keith shook his head. "All the other video portraits were done out here—Jeremy's and Tania's and Sandy's. I want them all to be in exactly the same place." Keith reached the top of the bleachers. "Besides, I told Cherise to meet us up here," he added. "Come on!"

Eva followed reluctantly. She really did not want to stand in front of a camera and talk, but she'd promised Keith.

"What should we talk about?" she asked.

"Whatever you want," he called over his shoulder. "Whatever's on your mind."

Tania and Sandy, Eva thought. *That's the only thing on anyone's mind.*

Tania and Sandy . . . and that horrible phone call yesterday.

Your turn next.

Eva shivered and ran up the last few steps, to join Keith at the top of the bleachers. While he checked out the camera, she fished in her jeans pocket, hoping to find a rubber band.

Nothing but lint.

"I can't stand this!" she cried, sweeping her hair out of her eyes.

Keith glanced at her. "Not your hair again."

"No!" Eva knelt down and began rummaging through her book bag. "It's not my hair at all. It's everything that's going on. I can't stop thinking about it!"

Keith carefully lowered the camera onto a bleacher seat. "Yeah. I know what you mean. I guess that phone call really shook you up, huh?"

"I'm scared to death," Eva admitted. She pawed through the book bag some more and finally found a rubber band way at the bottom. "That voice—I kept hearing it in my head, all night long."

"I wish I could have heard it," Keith said.

"You wouldn't have recognized it," Eva assured him. "It's creepy and rough. Not anybody we know." She grabbed her hair and twisted the rubber band around it. "Someone is planning to kill us all. But why? What did we do?"

Keith shook his head. "I don't know. I'm as confused as everybody else. We're all in the dark about this. That's what's so scary."

Eva took a deep breath. "Well, anyway, that's why I don't feel like doing the video—because I'm worried. Not because of my hair."

"But you'll do it anyway. Right?" Keith asked.

Eva nodded.

"Great." He picked up the camera and peered through the lens. "Smile—I'll make you a star."

I don't want to be a star, Eva thought.

I just want to be safe. I want everybody to be safe.

But she forced a smile. *Keith is only trying to cheer me up,* she realized.

"Okay . . . ready?" he called.

"Wait a sec." Eva glanced around. "I thought you said Cherise was coming."

"Yeah, well, she's late." Keith shrugged. "I'll get her some other time. Now—start talking."

Eva rolled her eyes. "Okay. Hi, Keith." She stuck out her tongue and waved to the camera. "How's that? Is that enough?"

"Are you going to clown around the whole time?" he asked, exasperated.

"Okay, no more clowning. I promise." Eva took a deep breath. "Hi. I'm Eva Whelan."

"Hold it," Keith interrupted. "Step back, would you? Lean against the bleacher rail. You look like you're standing at attention."

Eva backed up a couple of steps and stretched her arms out along the wooden railing.

"Perfect," Keith told her. "But lean against it. Try to relax."

Eva leaned back, letting the rail take most of her weight.

A horrible cracking sound split the air.

Gasping, Eva felt herself falling backward as the rail started to give way behind her.

"Help! Keith!"

Too late. She started to fall.

Out of the corner of her eye, Eva caught a glimpse of the ground, far below.

It really is *my turn,* she realized.

My turn to die!

23

"Keith!" Eva shrieked. "Keith!"

Eva twisted sideways and caught the edge of the bleacher step with one hand. She hung by an arm, her legs dangling in the air.

Her fingers began to slip. She screamed again.

Then Keith grabbed hold of her wrist, clamping onto it like a vise.

Eva swept her other arm toward him, and he latched on to that one too.

"Don't let me fall!" she cried. "Please!"

Keith began pulling her up, his eyes squeezed almost shut with the effort.

Pain shot through Eva's arms. It felt as if they were being torn from their sockets.

"Swing your leg up!" Keith groaned, pulling hard. His face turned red as he struggled to hang on. "Get your leg up!"

Eva's chest scraped against the edge of the bleachers. She swung her leg and tried to hook her toe onto the edge. But her sneaker started to slip off.

She bent her knee and felt it scrape up and over the rough cement. Keith pulled harder, grunting and straining.

And then she was up, scrambling over the edge.

She lay flat on her stomach on the hard cement, dazed with relief.

Keith sat back on his heels, panting.

Eva finally pushed herself to her hands and knees. "Thanks," she said shakily. She rolled over and sat. "Thanks, Keith."

"Sure." Keith hung his head, still catching his breath. "What happened, anyway? I heard this cracking sound."

"The railing. It broke."

Keith shook his head. "How could that happen? It's new. They put it in last spring, remember?"

Eva turned to the broken railing. It had broken in the middle, but it hadn't fallen completely off.

And the break didn't look jagged at all. It looked as if it had snapped cleanly.

After scrambling to their feet, they both went to check it out.

"It didn't break." Keith rubbed his finger

across one end of the wood, then stared at Eva. "This didn't break by itself. Somebody sawed it."

A shiver ran up Eva's back. She stared at the railing.

Someone tried to kill me, she realized.

And they almost succeeded.

"Come on." Keith's voice sounded rough with fear. "Let's get out of here."

He picked up his camera and started down the steps.

Eva followed, still shaken.

Your turn next, the voice had told her.

First Tania. Then Sandy. Then you.

Am I really next on the list?

Will someone try again?

When they reached the ground, Keith turned to her. "Are you really okay?"

"Sure. What about you?" Eva asked. "I mean, your arms must be about five inches longer."

Keith smiled grimly. "I'm fine."

"Good. But I lied before," Eva confessed. "I'm not okay. I'm scared."

"Yeah. Should we tell the police about it?"

"I guess." Eva sighed. "But what if they still think this whole thing is one big joke?"

"Wait until they see that railing," Keith declared. "That will show them. When they see that it was sawed, they'll know this is serious. Besides, after Sandy's murder they have to know this isn't a joke."

Eva nodded, swallowing nervously. *Serious is right,* she thought. *I almost fell and broke my neck.*

I could have died.

I was supposed to die.

Eva shivered. She glanced back up, to the top of the bleachers.

Someone stood there, not far from the broken railing.

"No! I don't believe it!" Eva screamed. "*You're* here?"

24

"Tania?" Eva shouted. "Tania!" The figure turned, her straight blond hair blowing in the wind.

"It *is* her!" Keith yelled. "Hey, Tania!"

Tania raised her hand in a quick wave, then started down the steps.

Eva couldn't wait for Tania to climb all the way down. With Keith behind her, she raced up the steps and met her friend halfway up the bleachers.

"You're alive!" she cried, throwing her arms around Tania. "I'm so glad to see you. I can't believe it! You're alive!"

Keith put his arms around both of them. "Hey, this is really incredible!" he declared. "Everybody's been going nuts around here. What happened to you?"

Tania hugged them for a moment, then pulled away.

Tears streamed from her eyes. "I . . . I just heard the horrible news about Sandy. So I came home."

"But where *were* you?" Eva demanded. "How could you just disappear like that without telling anybody? What happened?"

Tania wiped her eyes. Then she crossed her arms and stared at them. "It was a joke," she declared.

"What?" Eva couldn't believe it. "Are you serious?"

Tania nodded.

"Whoa," Keith murmured. "Some joke, Tania. We didn't exactly think it was funny."

Eva felt a surge of fury. "But how could you do something like that?" she shouted at Tania. "It's sick! We all thought you were dead! Do you realize how awful we all felt?"

"It wasn't funny!" Keith repeated.

"No, but what all of you did to me wasn't funny either," Tania replied heatedly.

"Huh?" Keith's mouth dropped open. "What did we do?"

"You made a fool out of me," Tania told them. "Everybody did. All of you knew Sandy was sneaking around with Cherise."

Oh no, Eva thought. *Now I get it. She thought we were keeping it a secret from her.*

"You all knew," Tania repeated. "And not one of you told me." Her green eyes flashed at Eva. "Not even you, Eva. My best friend! I was so angry and so hurt, I decided to pay you back."

"But . . ." Eva suddenly thought of something. "Tania—*you* made those frightening phone calls?"

"Yes, I did. I was so hurt. I really wanted to pay you back." Tania stuck her hands into the pockets of her yellow windbreaker and hunched her shoulders against the wind. "I mean, you all made a fool out of me. In front of the whole school!"

Eva glanced at Keith. *He looks so uncomfortable,* she thought. *How long has he known about Sandy and Cherise?*

"Tania, we didn't mean to make you feel like a fool," Keith told her.

"Maybe not, but that's what happened," Tania insisted. "Everybody knew but me. I felt like a total idiot!"

"That's no excuse for playing such a dirty trick," Eva snapped. "Anyway, I planned to tell you."

"Well, you waited too long," Tania declared bitterly. "When Jeremy told me about Sandy sneaking around with Cherise, I couldn't believe it. Once I stopped crying, I got so angry. And that's when I decided to get even."

"Where were you all this time?" Eva asked

Tania. "I mean, were you just hiding at home?"

Tania shook her head. "That's what I was going to do. But Jeremy had a better idea. He cooked up the whole thing. Sandy was in on the first part—the strangling part. But he didn't know I was going to disappear. Anyway, I went to stay with my cousins in Waynesbridge. I told Mom and Dad not to worry, and *they* told the police I was perfectly okay."

"So that's why the cops stopped the investigation," Keith said. "No *wonder* they thought the whole thing was a joke. It was."

"It was a horrible, sick joke, Tania!" Eva declared angrily. "How could you do that to us? How could you put us through all that just because your boyfriend was cheating on you?"

"I couldn't help it!" Tania cried. "I was so hurt and upset. And I wanted to hurt and upset everyone else, especially Sandy. I wanted you guys to feel like fools, just the way I did!"

Eva glanced down, taking a deep breath. She *did* feel like a fool. And she still felt hurt and angry. Tania got even, all right.

But at least she's alive, Eva told herself.

"How long was this joke going to last?" Keith asked Tania.

"Just another day or two," Tania told him. "But then I heard about Sandy." Her eyes filled with tears again. "It's just horrible. I really cared about him. Even though he was a sneak," she added.

Eva hugged her again. As she did, the familiar cold, dark feeling surged through her. "You said this was Jeremy's plan?" she asked.

Tania nodded as she pulled a tissue out of her jacket pocket.

"The whole thing?"

Nodding again, Tania wiped her eyes.

"Well, where is he?" Eva demanded. "Why isn't he . . ." She stopped as the feeling became stronger.

Something is wrong. Horribly wrong.

"Eva?" Tania asked. "What's the matter with you?"

"Something's going on," Eva murmured.

Someone is in trouble.

As soon as the words popped into Eva's mind, she realized they were true. *It's not just some weird feeling this time*, she thought. *I can tell that somebody's in trouble.*

But who?

Shivering, Eva glanced around, then up into the bleachers. As her gaze rested on the broken railing, she froze.

Cherise, she thought.

Cherise was supposed to be here an hour ago. She promised Keith.

And Cherise wouldn't pass up a chance to be on camera.

Where is she?

"Eva?" Tania repeated. "Please. What is it? Why are you looking up there?"

Eva dragged her eyes away from the railing. "Cherise is in trouble," she declared.

"What do you mean?" Keith asked. "What kind of trouble?"

"I don't know!" Eva exclaimed. "I can feel it, though. Really strong. I can't explain it, but I know it's true. I just know it!" She turned and began running down the steps, and Keith and Tania followed.

I need a phone, she told herself. She had accidentally left hers in her locker. *Call Cherise.*

Hurry!

Eva jumped over the last two steps and onto the football field. Then she whirled around.

"Keith, give me your phone!" Eva said.

Keith handed it over, and Eva pulled up Cherise's contact information.

Her heartbeat hammered so loudly in her ears, she could hardly hear the phone ring.

And ring.

And ring.

After fifteen rings, Eva ended the call. "No answer."

"Let's go to her house," Keith said. "Come on. We'll take my van."

The three of them raced out to the parking lot and piled into Keith's black minivan. All the seats had been folded down except the driver's. Eva sat with Tania on the scratchy carpeting in the back, hunched next to a pile of cardboard boxes holding cables and microphones and other video equipment.

Keith peeled out of the lot, ignoring the speed bumps. The tires screeched as he swerved onto the street. A horn blared loudly.

"Stop driving like a maniac!" Tania told him. "We'll never get there if you're pulled over for a ticket."

"Sorry." Keith slowed a little and clutched the steering wheel nervously. "Eva got me spooked."

Eva huddled near the bouncing boxes, digging her fingernails into her palms. *Hurry!* she wanted to shout. *Don't worry about a ticket. Just get us there, fast!*

A few minutes later, Keith pulled the van onto Cherise's street and barreled toward her house. The van lurched to a stop at the curb, and Eva slid the side door open.

As she jumped down to the sidewalk, she heard a scream.

A wild, terrified scream.

A girl's scream, from inside Cherise's house.

25

"Oh no!" Tania gasped, jumping down beside Eva. "Eva, you were right!"

Keith leaped out of the van, clutching his precious camera in one hand.

Another scream pierced the air.

"Whoa," Keith murmured, his face turning pale.

"Hurry!" Eva cried. She took off across the lawn, the dry fall leaves crunching under her feet.

As the three of them raced up the porch steps, the girl screamed again.

Louder this time. More terrified.

Keith yanked open the rattling screen door, and Eva shoved the front door open.

"Help me!" the girl's voice shrieked. "Somebody—please help me!"

Cherise's voice.

With Keith and Tania close behind her, Eva

tore down the hall and burst into the living room.

Eva saw Jeremy race across the rug, heading for the dining room.

The toe of his sneaker caught on the rug. He stumbled sideways, and fell to the floor.

As he tried to scramble up, Eva could hear him gasping in fear.

A whimpering sound made Eva turn. She bit back a scream of her own as she stared.

Cherise crouched on the floor near the couch, her red hair tangled, her eyes wild with terror.

In one hand, she clutched a long-bladed butcher knife.

Eva's mouth opened in a horrified cry.

"He . . . he killed Sandy!" Cherise screamed. She rose to her knees, still clutching the knife.

Eva's heart stopped, then began racing, trying to pound its way out of her chest.

"Jeremy killed Sandy!" Cherise wailed. "And he tried to stab me! But I grabbed the knife away!"

Jeremy leaped up, panic in his face. "Get away!" he shouted at them. He leaped over a footstool and raced toward the dining room again.

"Stop him!" Cherise shrieked. "He's the killer! Stop him! He wants to kill all of us!"

Eva couldn't move.

Keith stood frozen, his fingers nervously clutching the camera.

"Jeremy!" Tania sobbed, racing after him. "Jeremy—why? Why did you do it?"

26

Stay away!" Jeremy warned.

With a cry, Tania jumped at him— and tried to grab hold of his windbreaker. Instead she rammed into his back and knocked him off balance.

Jeremy pitched forward, then fell straight down.

A horrible cracking sound echoed through the room as his head slammed against the corner of a low table.

He groaned once, then didn't move.

"Jeremy?" Tania gasped. She shook his shoulder and peered into his face. "He's knocked out."

"Thank goodness!" Cherise cried.

Eva helped Cherise onto the couch. Keith stood by, a stunned expression on his face. Tania stayed next to Jeremy, keeping one hand on his shoulder.

"Cherise, what happened?" Eva asked.

Cherise took a deep, shaky breath. She still held the knife, and stared at it in horror as she spoke. "He tried to stab me," she told them. "He said he was going to kill me!"

"But why?" Tania cried. "Why would Jeremy want to kill you?"

Cherise turned and stared at her. "For you, Tania. He wanted to get revenge for you—by killing Sandy and me."

Tania's eyes filled with tears.

"He said you were the first family he ever had," Cherise went on. "He said he couldn't stand to see you hurt."

Tania blinked. The tears spilled out and rolled down her cheeks.

Eva stared down at Jeremy.

He told me he got into some trouble at his old school, she remembered. *But he didn't say what. He didn't want to talk about it. He said it was all in the past.*

What kind of trouble? Eva wondered. *Murder?*

Was murder in Jeremy's past?

No, he'd be in prison, wouldn't he?

Unless he got away with it somehow.

Eva jumped as Cherise touched her arm. "He told me he was going to kill you too, Eva."

"Me?" Eva felt dizzy. "Why would he want to

kill me? I'm Tania's best friend. He knows that!"

"Yeah, and he doesn't like it one bit," Cherise declared. "Tania spends too much time with you, he said. He's jealous of you, Eva."

"But . . ."

"I told you what he said about family," Cherise reminded her. "Jeremy wanted Tania and his mom and dad all to himself. He didn't want anybody butting in, not even you, Eva. He's really crazy."

Eva shook her head, shocked.

"And that's why he sawed the bleacher railing," Cherise added. "To get rid of you. Thank goodness you didn't fall!"

Eva couldn't take her eyes off Jeremy. *He wanted to kill me,* she thought in horror. *The guy I have a crush on wanted to kill me!*

This can't be happening. It can't be!

Cherise clutched Eva's arm again. "We have to call the police!"

"No." Tania wiped her eyes. "I mean, he's my brother! And besides . . ."

"We have to!" Cherise insisted. "Haven't you been listening to me? He killed Sandy and he tried to kill me and Eva!"

Tania sat back. "It just doesn't make any sense," she murmured, staring at Jeremy. "How can he be a killer?"

The room felt warm, but Eva began to shiver. Cherise's words raced through her mind. *Jeremy's crazy. Jeremy sawed the railing.*

He wanted to get rid of you.

He's a killer.

Is he? Eva wondered desperately. *Is it really true?*

"The sooner we call the police, the sooner we'll all be safe," Cherise declared. "Keith, would you . . ." She stopped suddenly as a low moan echoed in the room.

Jeremy.

He groaned a second time. His fingers twitched. One of his feet wiggled. But his eyes stayed closed.

"Call the police!" Cherise whispered urgently. "Hurry—before he wakes up!"

Jeremy moaned again, louder this time. His hands curled into fists and his eyelids fluttered. "Get away," he mumbled. "Got to . . ."

Cherise's fingers dug into Eva's arm. "Please—"

Jeremy's eyes snapped open. Rolling to his side, he raised himself on one arm and stared at Cherise.

Cherise slid to the edge of the couch.

"No!" Jeremy shouted suddenly.

Cherise began to stand, but her feet got tangled with Eva's, and she fell back onto the cushion with a gasp.

"Stop her!" Jeremy yelled. "Don't let her get away!"

He scrambled up, swaying a little. Then he pointed across the room at Cherise. "She killed Sandy!"

27

He's crazy!" Cherise cried.

"She killed Sandy," Jeremy repeated, rubbing the side of his head. "She did it!"

Tania stared at him in shock.

Keith backed toward the door, carrying the camera.

Eva stood up slowly. Her gaze skipped back and forth between Jeremy and Cherise.

Cherise stayed on the couch, her face flushed.

An angry red bruise had appeared on the side of Jeremy's forehead. But his eyes were clear and they never left Cherise's face.

"He's crazy!" Cherise repeated. Her voice shook with fear. "Don't listen to him! He didn't say a word to me. He just broke into my house, carrying a knife. This knife! I tried to talk to him, to ask him what he was doing, but he didn't say anything. He just kept coming at me!"

Jeremy started to speak, but Cherise wouldn't let him. "He stormed in here like some kind of monster," she said. "Then he suddenly yelled, 'This is for Tania!' And he tried to stab me."

"That's a total lie!" Jeremy shouted. "That knife isn't mine—it's hers!"

"That's not true!" Cherise screamed. "Tania, please, call the police!"

"Go ahead, Tania," Jeremy agreed. "Call them."

Tania stared at him as if he *were* crazy.

"Don't worry," Jeremy assured her. "I'll tell them exactly what happened. I'll tell all of you. Don't you want to know the truth?"

"Don't listen to him," Cherise pleaded. "Please, we have to get him out of here. I'm afraid!"

"Afraid of what?" Jeremy asked. "You have the knife."

"And I'm not letting go of it either," Cherise cried. "Not while you're here."

Jeremy turned to Eva and the others. "Cherise called me and asked me to come over to her house," he told them. "A few seconds after I got here, she saw you guys piling out of Keith's van. And then she screamed."

"Because you were going to kill me," Cherise insisted angrily.

Jeremy ignored her. "I didn't know what was going on," he continued. "Then she screamed again and grabbed that knife off the coffee table. I was practically paralyzed."

Cherise tossed her head in frustration. "It's not true. It's not! What are you waiting for, Tania? Do you want us all to die?"

"Don't you want to know what happened next?" Jeremy asked. "She threw herself down on the floor and screamed again. She was posing with that knife, acting terrified. But I was clear across the room! Don't you get it? She was trying to make it look as if I tried to kill her!"

Jeremy raked a hand through his hair, wincing as his arm hit the bruise on his forehead. "That's when I finally unfroze and started to run. I didn't see you guys at first, but when I did, all I wanted was for you to get away."

"That's a lie! A lie!" Cherise stepped backward, bumped against the coffee table, and sat down hard. "Please! You can't believe him. It's a lie!"

As Cherise began to stand, Eva edged farther away from her and said, "No. Wait."

Cherise snapped her head toward Eva, her blue eyes startled. "Jeremy is telling the truth," Eva declared. "Cherise, I know you're lying."

28

Cherise stood up, shaking her head violently. "No! Why are you saying that, Eva? It's his word against mine. How can you . . ." She paused. "Wait a second. Is this another one of your stupid psychic flashes?"

"They're not stupid," Tania declared. "That's what made us come over here in the first place. Eva knew something was wrong. She felt it, and she was right."

Cherise rolled her eyes. "Oh, please! I don't believe in that garbage. And nobody else will either."

"It doesn't matter," Eva said. "I don't need to be psychic to know you're lying, Cherise."

Cherise's eyes narrowed. "What's that supposed to mean?"

"Tania already told us that it was Jeremy's idea for her to pretend to be dead," Eva explained. "That was his plan for Tania to get revenge—by playing a cruel joke on us."

"So?" Cherise asked.

"So Jeremy wouldn't murder Sandy," Eva went on. "He knew that Tania was already getting her revenge."

"Hey, that's right," Keith remarked. "Sandy was a total wreck, worrying about Tania."

Cherise bit her lip. "But—if it was Jeremy's idea, then why did he break in here and try to kill me?"

"I didn't," Jeremy insisted.

Eva nodded. "That's right—he didn't."

"How do you know that?" Cherise demanded.

"You say Jeremy didn't say a word to you? He just burst into the house and attacked you?" Eva asked.

"Yes!" Cherise cried. "That's the truth."

Eva stared hard at her. "But before, you told us that he said he would kill me, too. And how did you know about the bleacher railing?" she asked. "You just said you were sorry about the railing breaking. But how did you know about it?"

"What?" Cherise's face went blank for a moment. Then a deep flush spread across it. "The— the railing?" she stammered.

"What railing?" Jeremy asked, confused.

"See?" Eva said to Cherise. "Jeremy doesn't even know about the railing breaking off. So the only way *you* could know is if you sawed that railing yourself!"

"Whoa," Keith murmured.

Eva kept staring at Cherise. "You did it, didn't you?" she asked. "You sawed the railing and you made everything else up!"

Cherise started to say something, then stopped.

"Admit it, Cherise," Eva insisted.

"Yes, admit it," Tania agreed. "Stop accusing my brother of trying to kill you!"

"Okay, okay!" Cherise cried. "I sawed the railing." She sat down on the coffee table again, holding the knife in her lap. "Feel better now, Eva?" she asked bitterly.

"Why? Why did you do it?" Eva shrieked.

"Oh, please—drop the innocent act!" Cherise tossed her head, glaring around the room. "I hate you all! You think you're so smart! Hey, let's keep a secret from poor, dumb Cherise. Won't that be a kick? The way you were laughing at me behind my back. Don't think I didn't catch on!"

"Catch on to what?" Jeremy asked.

"Keith's other video project—the candid video project, as if you didn't know," Cherise sneered.

"Huh?" Tania cried. "What video project?"

"You all knew that Sandy *pretended* to like me—just for the candid video," Cherise went on. "You all humiliated me, laughed at me—just for a stupid video!"

"What candid video?" Jeremy demanded.

Eva turned to Keith, totally confused. "Keith? What is she talking about?"

Keith adjusted his camera, not meeting their eyes. "Cherise is right," he admitted finally. "Sandy and I were secretly making another video."

"And everybody knew about it but me!" Cherise cried.

"Wrong," Keith told her. "Only Sandy and I knew about it. I had the camera hidden. Sandy was pretending to like Cherise. But it wasn't real. It was all for the video."

Cherise burst into tears.

Keith turned away, ashamed.

"I thought Sandy really cared about me," Cherise sobbed. "I thought he really loved me. But it was all an act. All for a stupid video!"

Eva felt awful for Cherise. "You killed Sandy, didn't you?" she asked softly.

Cherise nodded, still crying. "I was so humiliated. So furious! Yes, I killed Sandy. I murdered him!"

Tania gasped. Jeremy put an arm around his sister's shoulders.

Eva let out a shaky sigh. *At least we know,* she thought. *At least it's over.*

Cherise took a deep breath and wiped the tears off her face. "Then, after I killed him, I decided to go after the rest of you. I'd make you sorry for laughing at me. For ruining my life. I'd pay you back, one by one. You were next, Eva. When Keith said you'd be up in the bleachers today, I sawed the railing."

Eva shuddered, remembering that terrifying moment when she was hanging by her fingertips.

"Next would be Leslie. Or maybe Keith. I hadn't decided," Cherise went on. "But I figured I could pin the blame on Jeremy by saying that he tried to kill me, too."

She laughed bitterly. "I didn't know that Jeremy and Tania had cooked up her disappearance. I didn't know that Tania already told you guys that Jeremy was in on the joke."

No one spoke for a minute.

Then Eva turned to the others. "Let's call the police," she said softly.

"What good will that do?" Cherise asked. She'd stopped crying, and her eyes had turned cold. "You don't have any proof that I killed Sandy."

"Are you kidding?" Jeremy asked. "You just told us."

"So? Why should anyone believe you instead of me?" Cherise demanded. "Especially when you don't have a single way to prove it. I'll deny it all. And it's my word against yours."

Keith cleared his throat. "I'm afraid you're wrong, Cherise."

Eva turned to him, surprised.

"Oh?" Cherise asked coldly. "Exactly how am I wrong, Keith?"

Without a word, Keith held the camera up and tapped it with a fingernail.

Cherise's face drained of color.

"Yeah, you get the picture now, don't you?" Keith asked her. "I've had the camera turned on the whole time. I have your whole confession recorded."

Tania sighed with relief. "Thank goodness!"

Cherise jumped to her feet, scattering a stack of magazines onto the floor. "Give me that camera, Keith!"

"Sorry, Cherise. No way." Keith began backing toward the door.

Cherise raced ahead and beat him to it, blocking his path. "Give it to me!" she shouted.

Eva took a step toward her.

Cherise slashed the air between them with the knife.

Eva stopped, terrified.

Cherise swung back toward Keith. "Give it to me, Keith." She advanced on him, raising the knife. "You're not leaving the house with it. I swear you're not!"

Cherise raised the knife higher.

"Cherise!" Tania shrieked.

Jeremy kicked the magazines out of the way and raced across the room.

Eva reached out, trying to grab Cherise's arm.

Too late.

With a furious scream, Cherise plunged the knife toward Keith's chest.

29

Noooo!" Jeremy bellowed.

Tania and Eva both screamed.

Keith raised the camera to shield himself.

The knife clattered against the metal casing of the camera.

And bounced out of Cherise's hand. It landed on the living room rug.

With a cry of anger, Cherise whirled around and dove for it.

Eva kicked it away from Cherise's grasping fingers.

The knife spun across the rug, skidded under a chair, and banged up against the far wall.

Furious, Cherise turned back to Keith and swung her fist at the camera.

Keith shifted the camera to his other hand, raising it out of her reach.

"Give me that!" Cherise shouted. "Give it to me!" She drew her arm back, ready to swing again.

Jeremy caught her by the wrist, spun her around to face him, and grabbed her by the shoulders. "Stop it!" he shouted into her face. He shook her, hard. "It's over, Cherise. It's over!"

Cherise struggled, screaming and trying to hit him.

Keith set the camera down and helped Jeremy drag her to the couch. When they pushed her down, she collapsed against the cushions, sobbing in fury.

But she didn't try to get up.

Jeremy and Keith backed away from the couch, breathing hard.

Cherise curled her feet up and buried her face in one of the pillows.

Eva slowly let her breath out. *It finally* is *over,* she thought. She turned to Jeremy.

Still breathing hard, he held his arm out.

Eva hurried to his side and hugged him. Tania joined them. Then Keith slung his arms around the whole group.

They stood that way for a moment, shocked and relieved.

Keith finally broke the hug. "Now what?" he asked in a shaky voice.

Eva turned to the couch. Cherise still lay curled up, her face in the pillow, crying softly.

Eva sighed. "Now we call the police," she told him sadly.

When the two police officers arrived a few minutes later, Cherise had stopped crying. She sat stiffly on the couch, staring straight ahead, while the others explained what had happened.

The officers were the same ones who had come when Tania disappeared. One sat in a chair near the couch, writing in a small spiral notebook. The other stood behind the couch, listening.

They know part of the story, Eva thought. *But not the worst part. Not the part about Sandy.*

"Cherise was trying to get back at us," Eva told them. She sat on a footstool near the policewoman's chair. "She thought we were laughing at her behind her back. She sawed the bleacher railing so I'd fall. You can go check it out. But before that . . ." She paused.

The policewoman glanced up from her notebook. "Before that?"

"She killed Sandy Bishop," Tania said. "And she was going to kill Eva and Keith. And blame Jeremy for everything."

The policewoman gazed at Cherise. "Is that what happened, Cherise?"

Cherise shrugged.

"Is that a yes or a no?" the woman asked.

"It's a yes," Keith declared. He sat cross-legged near the door, holding his camera. "Cherise admitted that she killed Sandy, and all the other stuff too. We have her confession."

Both officers shifted their gaze to him.

Keith hoisted the camera. "It's all recorded."

The policewoman stared at the camera for a moment, then turned back to Cherise. "Is this true?" she asked.

Cherise started to shrug again. Then her shoulders sagged and she let her breath out in a long sigh.

Finally she looked at the police officer. "Yes. I might as well admit it." She gazed at the camera, and her mouth twisted in a bitter smile.

The officer finished writing and snapped her notebook closed. "Where are your parents?" she asked Cherise. "We have to call them. Then we'll take you down to the station."

"They're at a business convention downtown." Sighing again, Cherise rose to her feet. "The number is on the refrigerator door."

While the policeman followed Cherise to the kitchen, the other officer carefully placed the knife into a plastic bag. Then she turned to the others. "We're going to need statements from all of you," she told them. "Come down to the station tomorrow and we'll write them up for you to sign."

The officer and Cherise returned from the kitchen. "I made the call," the man informed his partner. "Her parents will meet us there."

"Right. Let's go." With a nod to Eva and the others, the policewoman strode out of the living room. Her partner followed, his hand wrapped around Cherise's arm.

At the living room door, Cherise stopped and gazed back at them.

Eva stared at her. *What should I do?* she wondered. *Wave goodbye? Wish her good luck? What do you do when someone you know turns out to be a murderer?*

But before Eva could do anything, Cherise walked quickly through the doorway.

"That was awful," Tania murmured with a shiver as they heard the front door slam shut.

Keith suddenly scrambled to his feet. "The cops forgot to take the camera!" he cried. "It has the recording on it!"

Clutching the camera, Keith dashed out of the living room and down the hall.

He was back a few seconds later, still holding the camera. "They already left," he announced.

"It's okay. We can take it to them," Eva told him. "But before we do, let's look at it."

"Good idea," Keith agreed. Everyone gathered around as he navigated to the saved video.

"I hope the thing is in focus," he muttered as he joined the others across the room. "It was starting to get dark. But I didn't want to do anything to stop Cherise from talking."

"Sshh," Tania told him. "It's starting."

A blue screen appeared.

Everyone waited.

But the screen remained.

Eva and Keith exchanged glances. "I don't believe it!" he cried. "It malfunctioned again."

Read on for a peek
at Fear Street:

THE WRONG NUMBER

1

THE FIRST WEEK IN SEPTEMBER

The blob of green gel oozed like something from the bottom of a decaying swamp. It spread and settled in its container, quivering, as if searching for a way to escape or a way to take over.

Deena Martinson plunged her hand into the porcelain sink and slowly squeezed the gelatinous mass.

"Yuck!" she said. "Are you sure you want to put this on your hair?"

"Go ahead," said her friend Jade Smith. Jade was sitting on a wooden stool in front of the bathroom mirror, a towel covering her shoulders, her freshly washed auburn hair hanging in damp coils down her back.

"I know your mom's a professional hairdresser," said Deena, "but this stuff looks like the thing that ate Cincinnati. And I won't even tell you what it feels like."

"Go on," Jade insisted. "My mom uses it on her hair all the time, and it looks great. All shiny and full of body."

"Are you sure you don't mean *dead* bodies?" cracked Deena. She began applying the gel to her friend's hair. Soon the long tresses were covered with slime and gave off a faintly Jell-O-y scent.

"Now what?" she asked when she had finished.

"Now we wait for it to dry," said Jade. "At which point I'll be ravishing. Sure you don't want to try it? We could do your hair in spikes."

Deena fingered her own baby-fine hair. It was shortish, and blondish, and straightish. All she could do was wear it layered and hope for the best. Her mother said her hairdo made her look like an angel. She wasn't sure she liked that idea, but spikes didn't sound any better. "No, thanks," she said. "I have enough problems without trying secret formula x-oh-nine or whatever it is."

"It could be your big chance," said Jade, but she didn't push. She didn't seem to care much. In fact, she sounded a little bored—as bored as Deena felt.

"What a way to spend Saturday night," said Deena with a sigh.

"Yeah, I hate to admit it," said Jade, "but I'll actually be glad when school starts Monday. It'll be great to see all the kids, start going to dances and games."

"Yeah, I guess," said Deena.

"Hey, Miss Enthusiasm."

"It's just I don't know what to expect," Deena said. "Things are going to be different."

"What do you mean?"

"I just found out that my brother, Chuck, is going to be living here."

"Your brother? You don't have a brother," said Jade.

"My half brother, actually. He's my dad's son from his first marriage. I've only met him a few times. He's coming to Shadyside for his senior year."

"Really?" Jade was all ears now, but then she usually was where boys were concerned.

"Down, girl," said Deena. "Chuck is nothing but trouble. In fact, that's why he's coming here. He was supposed to graduate from Central City last year, but he got expelled. His mom and my dad decided he'd do better in a small town like Shadyside."

"Expelled?" said Jade. "What for?"

"I'm not sure," said Deena. "It had something to do with some kids he hung out with. He actually got arrested one time. He's been getting in trouble ever since he was little."

"He sounds interesting," said Jade with a mischievous smile.

"To you, Freddy Krueger would sound interesting," cracked Deena, wandering into her bedroom.

"It's just that the regular boys at Shadyside are so predictable," said Jade, following her. "That's 'predictable,' spelled B-O-R-I-N-G." She pulled the towel off her shoulders, then shook her damp hair out and pirouetted in front of the full-length mirror on Deena's closet door, admiring her figure. She was wearing a pink-and-white-checked jumpsuit with short sleeves. Deena had heard that redheads weren't supposed to wear pink, but Jade looked good in every color of the rainbow—and she knew it. In fact, she was very vain. But, Deena had to admit, Jade had a lot to be vain about.

"How's your hair doing?" Deena asked to change the subject.

"Still cooking," said Jade. She suppressed a yawn, then sat on Deena's bed and began using an emery board on her already perfect nails. She looked around the room, and her eyes stopped on a bright blue plastic object on the bedside table.

"What's this?" she said.

"My new phone," said Deena. "When my dad

got promoted to vice president of the phone company, they gave us the latest instruments."

"It's pretty rad," said Jade, picking it up. "It looks like the control panel for a jet plane or something. What are all these buttons for?"

"They're for programming in phone numbers," said Deena. "You push one button, and the phone automatically dials a number. That button's for putting the caller on hold. And this switch"—she pointed to a switch on the handset—"turns it into a speakerphone, so everyone in the room can hear the conversation."

"Yeah?" said Jade. "That sounds like it has possibilities. In fact, it gives me an idea. Whose numbers are in it?"

"I haven't programmed in too many yet," said Deena. "Just my grandmother, Mrs. Weller next door, and you, of course."

"Me? Really? How do I dial it?"

"Just punch number three."

"Watch this. My little sister Cathy's babysitting the kids tonight." She punched number three, then flipped the switch for the speaker, a strange smile on her face.

"Hello," she said, holding her nose so she sounded as if she had a cold. "Miss Cathy Smith, please."

"This is Cathy Smith," said the voice on the other end. Through the speaker her voice sounded hollow and far away, as if it were coming from the bottom of a well.

"I'm calling from the Shadyside Mall Association," said Jade, still holding her nose. "Miss Smith, I regret to inform you that you have been selected worst-dressed shopper of the month."

"What?" shrieked Cathy at the other end. "I didn't even go to the mall today!"

"You were positively identified by over a dozen shoppers," said Jade. "You have exactly one hour to pick up your prize, a dozen wilted daisies."

"A dozen what?" wailed Cathy. Then her voice turned suspicious. "Wait a minute. I know who this is. It's not the mall. Jade, I know you—"

"I don't know what you're talking about," said Jade, pinching her nose even tighter. "This is the—"

"You can't fool me," Cathy went on. "Next time pick on someone as stupid as you are!" The sound of the click as she hung up filled the room.

"Rats!" said Jade. "I should try it with someone who doesn't know my voice so well. Someone who would never expect—I've got it! Deena, look up Henry Raven's phone number."

"Henry Raven?" said Deena. "He's such a nerd!

All he cares about is his computer. Why do you want to talk to him?"

"Just watch," said Jade. "Or rather, listen—to this!" She took the phone book from Deena, looked up the number, and punched in seven digits. The sound of a ringing phone filled the room, then a click, and then the unmistakable voice of Henry Raven.

"Hello?"

"Hello, is this Henry?" Jade was talking so low, she was almost whispering, and Deena thought her voice sounded mysterious and sexy.

"This is Henry," said Henry. "Who is this?"

"You don't know me, Henry," whispered Jade, "but I've had my eye on you for a long time." She whispered "long" so it sounded like "lo-o-o-ng," her voice breathy and seductive.

"Who *is* this?"

"Someone . . . who'd like to be a good friend. I like your style, Henry—"

"Is this some kind of a joke?"

"It's no joke," said Jade. "I've never been more serious. You're just the kind of guy a girl like me yearns for. . . ."

There was a long silence at the other end. Then suddenly Henry sputtered, "Find another guy! I don't have time for this!" And he hung up the phone with a bang.

Both girls fell onto the bed, laughing hysterically.

"Did you hear that? He doesn't have *time*!" Deena couldn't stop giggling.

"That was even better than I expected," said Jade when she stopped laughing. "Now it's your turn."

"My turn?" said Deena.

"Sure. You heard me. We'll just pick—"

"Jade, no!" said Deena. "I can't even talk to people in person!"

"That's the whole point," said Jade. "It's much easier when you're anonymous. Now, let's see," she went on, flipping through Deena's phone book. "How about Rob Morell?"

"Rob Morell?" shrieked Deena. "He's one of the most popular boys in the whole school!"

"So what?" said Jade. "You like him, don't you?"

"Sure," said Deena, "but when he was in my geometry class last year, I could never think of anything to say to him."

"Well, now's your chance," Jade said.

"But what if he finds out it's me?"

"Just whisper, like I did, and he won't have a clue," said Jade. Ignoring Deena's continuing protests, she punched in the number and thrust the phone at her friend.

"But what'll I *say*?" cried Deena, looking horrified.

"Whatever comes to your mind," said Jade. "Just be sexy."

"Hello?" squeaked Deena. Then she took a deep breath and dropped her voice. "May I speak to Rob Morell, please?"

Great! Jade mouthed the word. After a moment a sleepy-sounding boy's voice came over the speaker: "Hello?"

"Hello, Rob?" whispered Deena, making her voice as seductive as possible. "What's a good-looking guy like you doing home on a Saturday night?"

"Watching some movies," Rob said. "Who is this?"

"This is your secret admirer," said Deena. The words just came to her.

"My what? What's your name?"

"I can't tell you my name, because then it wouldn't be secret anymore." Deena was amazed at herself. So far the words came easily, as if she were reading them from a script.

"Well, if you can't tell me your name, tell me what you look like," said Rob. He no longer sounded sleepy. In fact, he was sounding interested!

Deena shut her eyes and leaned back on the bed. "What do I look like?" she repeated. "Well, I'm about five four, one hundred and five pounds, with blond hair to my waist. My eyes are green, and I have full lips."

"Say, maybe we could get together sometime," said Rob.

"I'd like that," said Deena. "You're such a good-looking guy. I'll call you again one night real soon."

"How about tonight?" said Rob. "Or tomorrow? Can I have your number?"

"I've got to go now," said Deena. "Remember, I'll call again."

She leaned forward and hung up the phone, then looked at Jade a moment. They collapsed back onto the bed, shrieking with laughter. "He bought it!" cried Deena. "I can't believe it! He was practically drooling!"

"You were great!" said Jade. "You're a natural. He'll probably stay home waiting by the phone for the next month!"

"You were right," said Deena. "It was easy. Much easier than talking to someone in person."

"I told you so," said Jade. "So who should we call next? How about—"

"Not tonight," said Deena, looking at her

watch. "It's getting late, and my folks will be home any minute."

"What about tomorrow?" said Jade.

Deena shook her head. "Tomorrow night my dad and I are driving to the airport to pick up my brother, Chuck."

"Be sure to tell him hello for me," said Jade.

"He doesn't even know you."

Jade turned her full smile on. "Not now he doesn't," she said. "But I have a feeling . . . he will soon."

2

On the way to the airport Deena felt both excited and nervous. She was beginning to like the idea of having a long-lost brother in the house. In fact, she realized, there could be certain important advantages—such as he could introduce her to his friends. Then she remembered everything she'd heard about the trouble Chuck had been in. She got a funny feeling in the pit of her stomach that maybe things weren't going to work out so well.

Also, her father seemed really nervous, even more nervous than she was.

"Be friendly to him, Deena," her dad said. "But try to give him space. Remember, he grew up in a big city and isn't used to small-town friendliness."

"Right," said Deena. *He'll probably think we're all a bunch of hicks,* she thought.

Her first glimpse of Chuck was promising.

She hadn't seen him since he was about ten, and he'd grown up since then. He was tall now, and his T-shirt and tight jeans showed off the taut muscles of an athlete. His hair was thick and sandy-colored above startlingly blue eyes. Jade, Deena knew, would call Chuck a hunk. But when she got closer, she saw that something was wrong with the picture of the all-American good-looking guy.

For one thing, there was the expression on his face.

Deena wasn't sure what it was. It seemed to be somewhere between a sneer and a scowl. *A snowl?* she wondered.

When Deena's father put out his hand for a handshake, Chuck pretended he didn't see it. Mr. Martinson looked a little flustered and smiled uncertainly. "Chuck, you remember your sister, Deena."

Chuck looked at her as if she were a toad or some other low form of life. "Hello, kid," he said.

Kid? This year was going to be awful, Deena knew. But in the next instant Chuck smiled at her, a goofy, lopsided smile that made him look like a completely different person. She smiled back nervously, wondering what to expect next.

On the way home it was even more confusing. Deena sat in the back seat and listened while her father and Chuck talked.

Except it was mostly her father talking. Chuck just grunted. Once he said, "This is such a drag, man. I don't see why I can't go back to Central City High."

"Because they won't let you back in," said Mr. Martinson. "Your mother and I have repeatedly talked to them, as you well know." For the first time Deena's father sounded a little exasperated, maybe even angry. Deena hoped to hear more about why Chuck had been expelled. "I want to make clear to you—" her father started.

But the sound of squealing brakes and screeching tires interrupted him.

Deena screamed at the sound of the crash.

She heard glass shattering. Then another crash.

A horn started honking, then another. Someone cried out.

More tires squealed. Deena held her hands over her ears.

Mr. Martinson, a look of horror on his face, his mouth wide open, stomped on the brakes. His tan BMW skidded toward a jumble of other cars and came to a stop just inches from the car in front of it. Behind them Deena could hear more cars sliding and skidding. "Get out!" Mr. Martinson ordered. "It'll be safer outside the car!"

Deena and Chuck quickly scrambled out onto

the grassy shoulder and away from the pile of cars. Up above, a million stars were sparkling in the sky. Chuck began to trot toward the crowd at the front of the traffic jam. Deena followed him out of curiosity.

"Hey—come back!" her father yelled. Chuck ignored him and kept jogging. Deena hesitated, looked back at her father, then followed Chuck.

At the head of the tangle of cars, a red Plymouth sat crumpled against the concrete divider, smoke pouring out of its engine. While Deena and Chuck watched, flames began to lick up from the bottom of the car toward the doors.

"Look out!" someone shouted. "It's on fire!"

The crowd began to move back. Deena watched with horror as the fire began to grow. She edged back even farther on the shoulder, to get as far away from the car as possible. All at once she noticed that Chuck wasn't with her. He was standing at the front of the crowd, staring at the flames as if he was hypnotized.

Suddenly there was a brokenhearted scream from the crowd. "Tuffy's in there!"

Deena turned to look and saw a young boy holding a bloody towel to his forehead. "Tuffy!" the boy called. "Save Tuffy!"

"There's a dog in the car!" someone else

shouted. And now Deena could see the face of a small black-and-white dog at the back window. The dog was jumping up and down, barking hysterically.

The flames licked higher and higher.

Someone broke loose from the crowd and began running toward the burning Plymouth.

"No!" shouted a man in the crowd. "It's going to blow up!"

The figure kept running, then disappeared into the thick smoke.

To her horror, Deena realized it was Chuck.

"Chuck! Chuck! Come back!" she shrieked.

But she was too late.

The car exploded in a blazing fireball of red and orange flames.